AMBUSHED . . .

"Get down," Slocum yelled. "They're behind those rocks. This way!" Slocum shoved his Colt Navy back into his holster.

"You winged one of the bastards!" cried Trey.

Slocum joined Trey behind the waist-high stack of cut wood. Splinters began flying all around them as the ambushers got down to serious shooting.

"We flushed someone out," Trey said. "Are they rustlers?"

"They're someone who wants us dead," Slocum said. "Doesn't much matter beyond that." He poked his head out for a quick look and took a bullet through the brim of his Stetson.

"What are we going to do?" Trey asked. "I have a rifle but not that much ammo. How about you?"

"Not enough for a full-fledged fight. We don't even know how many of them are out there."

"We can run for it. We'll have a clear run all the way back to the Sleepy K," said Trey.

"I don't like running from a fight," Slocum said.

Slocum considered their position and the seemingly endless supply of ammunition being blasted in their direction by the ambushers.

"So we rush them?"

"Why not?"

DON'T MISS THESE
ALL-ACTION WESTERN SERIES
FROM THE BERKLEY PUBLISHING GROUP

THE GUNSMITH by J. R. Roberts

Clint Adams was a legend among lawmen, outlaws, and ladies. They called him . . . the Gunsmith.

LONGARM by Tabor Evans

The popular long-running series about U.S. Deputy Marshal Long—his life, his loves, his fight for justice.

SLOCUM by Jake Logan

Today's longest-running action Western. John Slocum rides a deadly trail of hot blood and cold steel.

BUSHWHACKERS by B. J. Lanagan

An action-packed series by the creators of Longarm! The rousing adventures of the most brutal gang of cutthroats ever assembled— Quantrill's Raiders.

JAKE LOGAN

SLOCUM
AND THE WOLF HUNT

JOVE BOOKS, NEW YORK

SLOCUM AND THE WOLF HUNT

A Jove Book / published by arrangement with
the author

PRINTING HISTORY
Jove edition / December 1998

The Penguin Putnam Inc. World Wide Web site address is
http://www.penguinputnam.com

ISBN: 0-515-12413-3

A JOVE BOOK®
Jove Books are published by The Berkley Publishing Group,
a member of Penguin Putnam Inc.,
375 Hudson Street, New York, New York 10014.
JOVE and the "J" design are trademarks
belonging to Jove Publications, Inc.

PRINTED IN THE UNITED STATES OF AMERICA

10 9 8 7 6 5 4 3 2 1

1

Heavy gray haze filled the bowl in the dreary black mountains holding Bannock, Montana. Slocum took a deep breath and coughed from the pall of woodsmoke mingled with horse and human odors caught in the hot, still air of the late summer afternoon. Wiping sweat from his forehead, he came to a decision where to ride. Bannock was a mining town on the decline, but some riches from the silver still flowed through it. Still, Slocum wasn't sure he wanted to be around people right now.

Bad experiences down in Salt Lake City had soured him on rubbing elbows. At least for the time being. Still, after patting his shirt pocket and finding it puffed up only with fixings for a smoke and a few crumpled greenbacks, he knew he had to earn some money before traveling on. Seattle and its timber industry appealed to him. Or perhaps a horse breeder in Oregon could use Slocum's expertise in breaking Appaloosas. Slocum had always had an affinity for the magnificent, splotched animals.

Truth was, about anything was better than dealing with drunk miners and suspicious townspeople.

But the money. If he wanted enough to keep riding,

he had to find a way of earning a few more dollars. The ranches surrounding the town looked prosperous enough, and might afford Slocum some work, but the truth was he wanted to be alone on the trail, just him, his horse, and the sun and stars and summer breeze in his face.

Following the rough road down into the bowl where Bannock crouched like some ugly sore made him feel as if he were being swallowed by a giant with bad breath. The gray haze turned greenish and then yellow as sulfur fumes rose from a smelter at the far end of town, the thick clouds trapped under the heavier smoke.

By the time he reined back in front of the Quick Buck Saloon his throat was raw and he was ready for a drink. Just one, maybe a nickel beer, and then on to find a few days' work. Slocum entered the saloon and stopped inside the door, keen green eyes swinging from one side to the other. At this time of day the saloon was mostly empty. A few cowboys bellied up to the bar, nursing watered-down whiskey. At a green felt-covered table at the back of the long, narrow room sat a tinhorn gambler and three scruffy miners, from the look of their canvas pants and worn red-and-black-checkered shirts.

"Beer," Slocum ordered, dropping a dime on the bar. It rattled twice as it rocked to and fro, then settled down with a solemn finality. Slocum had too few of them to spend on luxuries.

"Never seen you here before," the barkeep said, shoving the frothy mug in Slocum's direction. He reached under the bar and brought out a plate of bread, cheese, and thick slabs of ham for Slocum to build himself a sandwich. Slocum tried not to appear too eager to wolf down the food. His belly rubbed up against his backbone and thought his throat had been cut. The food sank down nicely, washed away by the beer.

"Another?" asked the barkeep. "I know a hungry, thirsty man when I see one."

"One more," Slocum decided. The entire dime was gone. But he was feeling like he could whip the world now that the edge had been taken off his hunger and thirst.

"Bannock's not got much in the way of work right now," the barkeep said, as if reading Slocum's thoughts. "Been having some trouble."

"Mine closing?" guessed Slocum.

"Richest mines are closed," the barkeep agreed. "But there's more. The ranches are having their share of woe." Before Slocum could ask about this, the barkeep turned and smirked. "Just like those galoots are having their share of woe. They're too liquored up to know when they're bein' fleeced."

"The gambler's cheating them?" Slocum eyed the gambler in his fine brocade vest, split-tail broadcloth coat, and flashy tooled boots. He didn't miss the small pistol in the hidden shoulder holster, the knife at the nape of the man's neck, or the possible derringer or knife sheathed under the broad coat lapels.

The barkeep laughed and shook his head. "He don't have to. They're practically *givin'* away their money. Fool and his money are soon parted. Mark my words, that gambler's going to pocket danged near a thousand dollars before this day's over."

"Those miners have that much?"

"Sold their mine this morning to some big San Francisco mining conglomerate. They'll be broke by dawn tomorrow, if not sooner." The bartender polished away at a shot glass with a dirty rag, shaking his head and mumbling, "Drunk fools."

Slocum took his beer and walked to the table. The gambler sat with his back to the corner of the room. The three miners had no such self-preservation instinct. Slo-

cum watched the play a few minutes, and saw the barkeep's appraisal was accurate. The miners had no sense
of odds and bet wildly on bluffs. The gambler had a
slight twitch to his mustache that Slocum noted whenever the man held a poor hand and bluffed his way to
raking in the pot.

"Mind if I sit in?" Slocum asked.

"Why, pardner," boomed one drunk miner, "you're
just what this anemic game needs. Fresh blood! Lemme
buy you what you're drinking." He closed one eye and
bent forward, staring into the glass. Then he peered up
myopically at Slocum. "Don't tell me a gent like you's
drinkin' dog piss? Barkeep! Bring us another bottle of
that good stuff you h-hide under the back-bar." The
miner hiccupped and rocked back in his chair as the
bartender brought a full bottle. He glanced at Slocum,
winked, then left quickly.

Slocum looked around the table. The gambler glared
at him, angry at having anyone else move in on his territory. The other two miners were oblivious to Slocum
as the verbose one welcoming him to the game poured
each a shot of whiskey.

"Let's play," the gambler insisted.

Slocum had little in the way of a stake and bet carefully, slowly winning until he had almost a hundred dollars piled in front of him. The miners lost consistently
to the gambler, and never seemed to notice. Slocum's
few dollars were nothing compared to the gambler's
take. Play went slowly until Slocum found himself looking at a full house, sixes over treys.

The miners bet wildly, as they had earlier, drunker
than lords and having more fun than they should. When
they sobered the next morning and found themselves
stone broke their mood might be a mite more bleak, but
now they cooperated with Slocum. And the gambler.

Slocum saw the man's mustache twitch slightly, hint-ing he had a lousy hand and would be willing to bluff with it. Play went around the table, two miners dropping out, leaving only Slocum, the friendly miner, and the gambler.

"Now, gents, I been gettin' bad hands all day long," the miner said. "This time I got the best one ever. You might as well fold and let me figger how to spend my winnings." The miner smiled and clutched his cards to his chest like a mother nursing a newborn.

"See you," the gambler said. "Raise ten dollars."

Slocum checked and knew he was in this to the finish, in spite of his lack of reserves. All the money he had was now on the table in the pot. He watched the gambler. The mustache twitch got worse. Slocum wished he had another hundred dollars to clean out the tinhorn's stake.

"You gonna raise, son, or you gonna drop out?" asked the miner.

"I've got this watch," Slocum said, pulling out his brother Robert's only legacy to him. Robert had been killed during Pickett's Charge and this keepsake was all he had left, other than memories.

"No hardware," the gambler protested. "This is a greenbacks-and-gold-dust game."

"Aw, let him bet. Hell, he can't beat me!" the miner said, laughing, as he almost fell from his chair. He grabbed for the whiskey bottle and took a long pull on it. Slocum wondered if the miner could even focus his eyes by now, much less know a winning hand.

"I'm folding," said the gambler, dropping his cards onto the table.

Slocum sat up a bit straighter when one of the gambler's cards accidentally flipped over. A six of diamonds, the twin to the one in his hand.

"Let's see your cards, fella," said the miner.

Slocum showed his full house.

The miner laughed again and showed four kings. As he reached for the pot, including the precious pocket watch, Slocum grabbed the man's wrist and held him back.

"I want to look at the gambler's cards."

With his free hand Slocum turned over the cards and saw a second six matching another in his hand.

"Seems there are a powerful lot of sixes in this deck. Think the same's true of kings?"

The miner shoved hard against the table, knocking Slocum back. Slocum found himself watching four men going for six-shooters—and feeling like a damned fool. He hadn't been playing against the gambler. He had been playing against a team used to working together, three miners, the tinhorn, and probably the barkeep as well.

He had been lured into the game, and now felt the lash of the consequences for not being more cautious or less greedy.

In a quick movement, Slocum kicked the chair away and got his feet under him, hand poised over the butt of his ebony-handled Colt Navy. As fast as he was, he realized he would be ventilated in the wink of an eye if the lead started flying. The miners were not as drunk as they had let on, and the gambler could go for any of three or four weapons.

Slocum might have taken out the gambler or a pair of the miners, but he stood no chance against the four.

"Keep the money. I want the watch," he said.

"So do I," said the gambler. "Looks like a fine chronometer, and I been needin' one to replace a watch I lost on the trail."

"The watch and I walk away, no blood spilled," Slocum said coldly. He cursed himself for being such a fool. Not even a greenhorn would fall into such an obvious trap, yet he had. His instincts about avoiding settlements larger than a pair of bedrolls and a campfire had been good. If only he had listened to his inner voice and kept riding, leaving filthy Bannock far behind.

"We won, fair and square," the gambler said.

"There are too many sixes in this deck," Slocum said.

"So maybe you were cheating," the gambler said. "They string up men for that in these parts."

"The watch," Slocum said, fixing his gaze smack on the gambler.

"We've taken a real shine to that watch, yes, sir, we have," said the overly friendly miner. Slocum realized then who the leader of this swindle really was. The gambler was a cat's-paw and nothing more. Get the rube into the game, then the miners would fleece him.

"You willing to die for it?" Slocum asked.

"Are you?" the miner asked, steel in his voice now.

Before Slocum could say a word, a sharp crack echoed through the narrow room. Slocum cast a quick glance out of the corner of his eye in the direction of the door leading to Bannock's main street, and saw sunlight glinting off a battered badge.

"What's going on here?" Again came the sharp crack as the deputy smashed an oak ax handle down onto a table.

"Hey, stop that, Hines. You're gonna bust up the furniture," protested the barkeep.

"Shut your tater trap, Herschel," snarled the deputy. "I know what kind of place you run here." The deputy, a banty rooster of a man, strutted up, shoved out his chest, and thrust his chin in Slocum's direction. "What's the story?"

"Too many of the same cards on the table," Slocum said. He ignored the deputy, preferring to keep his eyes on the gambler in case gunplay started.

"I warned you boys about this before," Deputy Hines

said. He brought down the ax handle as the gambler reached for the telltale cards. With a quick motion, the lawman used the wood stick to turn over the cards. "You don't even cheat good, Horace," the deputy said in disgust. Then he turned and fixed his hot stare on the miner Slocum pegged as the ringleader.

"You been livin' on borrowed time around here, Maxim. You and your cronies ought to drift on out of town. Next time I might get riled and do something."

"*He* was the one cheating," Maxim said.

The deputy put a restraining hand on Slocum's chest and gently pushed him back.

"Don't go insultin' my intelligence, Maxim. Your cards, your friends, a barkeep who gets ten percent of everything you steal."

"Ten?" bellowed the barkeep. "They was only givin' me five. You mean they give the others ten percent?"

"Here's how we're gonna work this," Hines said. "Room and board for a night. Call it ten dollars. And the matter's settled."

"The watch," Slocum said. "I want the watch."

"No," Maxim said. "I've taken a fancy to the time-piece."

The deputy looked from Slocum to the miner and back. He took a deep breath and asked Slocum, "You'd swap ten dollars for the watch?"

Slocum nodded.

"Gentlemen, this is going to turn bloody if you don't go along with it. Give the man ten dollars . . . and his watch back. And get the hell out of Bannock! The sorry lot of you!"

The miner started to bring his fist down on Slocum's watch. A quick move by Slocum deflected the blow so that the hard fist hit the table and sent greenbacks flut-tering into the air. Slocum snared the watch and tucked it away safely, then picked through the money to get his ten dollars.

"Thanks," he said to the deputy, still not taking his eyes off the four men who had bilked him so easily.

"You run on along now, hear?" said Hines. "I'll deal with these four."

Slocum stepped into the hot afternoon dust and smoke, and immediately coughed again. He needed to find open country and fresh air. Most of all he ought to have his horse tended. Ten dollars wouldn't go too far, but it was more than he'd had in his pocket when he rode into town.

Boots clicking on the boards behind him caused him to swing around, his hand reaching for the six-gun in its cross-draw holster.

"Relax," the deputy said. "I gave them the what-for. You look like a smart man. Why'd you get suckered into that game?"

"Greed," Slocum said, pinpointing his exact motive. "And I wanted to get enough money so I could move on without having to stay in Bannock overlong."

"You are smart, except in the way you play," the deputy said. He hitched up his gunbelt and spat into the street. "You have the look of a gunfighter. That your profession?"

"No," Slocum said. "I break horses. I do other things too, but I'm no paid killer."

Slocum hoped this would satisfy the deputy. He had too many warrants following him throughout the West. Immediately after he'd returned to the family farm in Calhoun County, Georgia, after the war, he'd been beset by a carpetbagger judge who'd insisted that no taxes had been paid. Slocum's Stand had been in the Slocum family since George II had deeded it to them, and no Reconstruction judge was going to take it without a fight.

The judge and a hired gun had ridden out to seize the

property. Slocum had ridden away that afternoon, two new graves left behind the springhouse. Judge-killing, even killing crooked judges, carried a heavy penalty, and Slocum had spent years dodging that wanted poster.

"You have the steely eye of a man who's no stranger to seeing other men die," the deputy pressed.

"That's true," Slocum said. "What are you getting at?"

"Maybe nothing. I wasn't joking about you movin' on. You and them thieves back in the saloon are all better off far away from my jurisdiction. That way, we all live longer, happier lives." The deputy shoved out his chest and peered up at Slocum with a cold eye, then strode off, whistling a bawdy tune and never once looking back.

Slocum knew an ultimatum when he heard one. Get out of town or land in the hoosegow—or worse.

2

Slocum touched the ten dollars in his shirt pocket and felt a simmering anger, both at himself for being so gullible and at the deputy for running him out of town. Bannock wasn't an oasis by any means. Slocum had not even wanted to stop until the idea of a beer had come to him, but now that he had been told to leave, he perversely wanted to stay.

Two ragged cowboys climbed down from their horses and rubbed their butts, which told Slocum they had been in the saddle a long time. He sauntered across the street to talk to them.

"Howdy," he said. Both turned and looked at him as if he had stuck them with pins. Of all the reactions possible, this was far from the one he had expected. They looked spooked.

"Hello," said the taller of the pair. He wiped his lips using his forearm, getting caked dust off. But the move was more nervous than practical. The other cowboy's hand hovered near the hogleg thrust into his belt.

"I'm looking for a job. Anything available around here you gents know about?"

They exchanged glances, then relaxed. The taller one

11

spoke for them. "Jobs are going begging around here, unless you're damned stupid."

Slocum considered his brief history in Bannock. Being "damned stupid" fit right in with the way he had swallowed the hook and gotten reeled into the poker game.

"That's me," he said.

"Hungry or stupid?" asked the shorter one, a smile coming to his lips.

"A little of both. Got enough money for a room for the night and some grub. That's all."

"Stay out of the Quick Buck Saloon," the taller said, lifting his chin and pointing in the direction of the emporium where Slocum had met his match.

"Figured that one out for myself," Slocum said. "What I need is a job riding the range. I'm good at breaking horses, and can keep a herd together as good as the next man."

The tall man snorted, then spat. "Not many beeves needin' lookin' after now," he said. Slocum didn't understand. The cowboy shrugged and said, "There's no jobs around, not really. You're best off just headin' on out of Bannock."

"Be sure to keep a good fire going all night," the shorter cowboy said, his voice rising to a shrillness that told Slocum he was scared spitless.

"Why's that? Spooks?"

The cowboys exchanged glances again, then walked off without another word. Slocum started to call after them, then stopped. Something was going on in Bannock that frightened usually fearless men. Slocum walked down the street, finding the general mercantile. The owner sat inside, feet propped on the counter, reading a newspaper.

Slocum went in and looked around the small shop. He blinked when he saw the layout. The usual merchandise was pushed to one side of the store to make room for rack after rack of rifles and a stack of ammunition big enough to fight a small war. The owner dropped his feet and put down his newspaper, seeing Slocum's interest in the firearms.

"You have the look of a man who knows his way around a fine rifle," the shop owner said. He came over and pulled a rifle from the rack, opened it so Slocum could examine the chamber and barrel, and started with his sale pitch. "A Sharps .50 ought to bring down just about anything you'd find out there."

"It's a rifle better suited for killing a buffalo," Slocum observed. Most of the rifles on display were large-caliber, designed for hunting big animals. "There a lot of bear in these parts?"

"Bears? Well, sure, there are a few of the big grizzlies. Black bear, some sunburst bears—you know them, the ones with the small yellow mark on their chests."

"This is a big rifle for a small bear," Slocum said, handing it back to the store owner.

"If you prefer speed of shooting to stopping power, how about this beauty?" The storekeeper grabbed another rifle and loaded it, then cycled eight shells out in the span of a double heartbeat.

"Why'd you need to shoot that fast? Might melt the barrel," Slocum said, more curious than ever. "Blackfoot? Haven't heard of Indian trouble lately around here."

"You funnin' me, mister?" the owner asked, slamming the rifle back into the rack. "You going to buy something or are you just flapping your tongue to hear yourself talk?"

"I need a job and thought you might have heard of some spread around town looking for hands."

The owner laughed harshly and shook his head. "Nobody who hasn't been dropped on his pumpkin head would want to stay around here. You just ride on out of Bannock.''

This sparked a flare of anger in Slocum. Everyone told him to leave town. The deputy, the cowboys, the shopkeeper.

"I don't run," Slocum said.

"Then you're gonna get yourself killed," the man said hotly. "Now, either you buy something or you get on out of here!''

Slocum wondered again at the mountain of ammunition and enough rifles to arm an entire cavalry company, then left. He stepped out into the early twilight. A wind whipped down from where Slocum had entered town, causing some of the heavy smoke pall to stir and vanish into the gathering night. The coolness evaporated sweat from his forehead and invigorated him.

"You find a place to stay? The Chancellor Hotel at the edge of town's clean and cheap,'' said the deputy's voice from the shadows to Slocum's right. Hines stepped out into the pale yellow light cast by a gaslight a dozen yards away.

"Looking for a way to make a few dollars before moving on,'' Slocum said, challenging the deputy.

"Bannock's got problems right now, problems I don't see you helping solve one bit.''

"Robbery? Cattle rustling?'' Slocum guessed. "I talked to a couple cowboys earlier, and they didn't have much good to say about the town.''

"That'd be Silent Dan and his partner, Utah. Tall fellow is Utah.''

"Could be them, though the short one was anything but silent.''

The deputy pushed his Stetson back. "Times like these make even the quiet ones chatter like magpies.''

"What the hell's going on here?'' Slocum asked flat

out. "Everyone dances around the problem without giving a good notion of what it is."

Hines stared at him, then heaved a deep sigh. "I can tell you're not a man who lets loose of an idea easily. A real bulldog when it comes to trouble." He heaved another sigh. "You might ride on out to Frank Kincannon's spread, the Sleepy K. Ten miles out of town in that direction." The deputy pointed north. "Of all the ranchers, he might be the one looking for a man with special talents. You have the look of such a gent."

"What special talent might that be?" Slocum had to ask.

"Killing." With that, the deputy spat, turned, and walked slowly down the street in the direction of a saloon where a fight had spilled out into the street.

Slocum found the well-kept road leading into the Sleepy K just after sunrise. He sat astride his horse and stared in the direction of the comfortable ranch house. Everything about Kincannon's spread seemed well ordered and prosperous—except for the lack of hands out doing chores and riding the fences along the road. Slocum had seen a couple of places where the wire needed replacing.

He rode slowly toward the house, making sure anyone inside had a good long look at him. It never paid to surprise people.

By the time he swung his long leg over the back of his horse and settled onto the ground, a stocky man with graying hair and a potbelly hanging over his belt came out the front door. He paused a moment, as if resting a rifle against the wall just inside the door.

"Howdy," Slocum called. "I'm looking for Mr. Kincannon."

"You found him," the man said. "What's your business? We're not getting many travelers passing by these days."

Slocum explained how the deputy in Bannock had aimed him in this direction. "Folks are mighty close-mouthed about what trouble's brewing in these parts. Maybe you'll be more forthcoming."

"You looking for a job?" Kincannon asked. "Yes, I see you are. Come on inside. You eaten breakfast yet?"

"A bit of food would set well," Slocum admitted. He had spent almost all the ten dollars on dinner the night before and on the room and a hot bath. Breakfast had been a luxury he couldn't afford.

"The wife's fixing it now." Kincannon went back into the house. Slocum saw he was right about the rifle leaning against the wall by the door.

"Cora, this is—" Kincannon turned and looked at Slocum.

"John Slocum's the name, ma'am," Slocum said. The woman putting food on the table was considerably younger than Kincannon, or maybe the man had just lived a hard life.

"Cora Kincannon," she said quietly. She didn't smile.

"And I am Elspeth Kincannon," said a livelier voice. Slocum turned and saw a young woman pushing through the door, carrying a stack of plates. She was about the prettiest thing he had ever seen. Long, lustrous midnight-black hair tumbled back over her shoulders in soft waves. Tanned and lovely, she moved like an angel as she put plates around the table. She pointed to a chair across the table from hers, indicating Slocum should be seated.

"That's my daughter," Kincannon said. "And this is my brother, William."

A man the spitting image of Frank Kincannon came into the room. About the only difference between the brothers lay in the hair. William Kincannon hadn't gone gray and might have been ten years younger, about the same age as Cora Kincannon.

"What do you want?" William Kincannon said brusquely. "We're not looking for any more hands right now."

"Will, button your lip," Kincannon said harshly. "You are always putting the cart before the horse."

"We can deal with the trouble ourselves. We don't need outsiders coming in and—"

"And what?" Slocum asked. "If you think I'm intruding, I'll leave right now. Thanks for your hospitality," Slocum said, pushing back from the table.

"Uncle Will, you can be so rude!" flared Elspeth. "Please, Mr. Slocum, sit down. We *do* need men. Are you a hunter?"

"Beg your pardon?" The question puzzled him.

"You have the look of a man who is good with a six-shooter," Frank Kincannon said. "Are you any good with a rifle?"

Slocum had been a sniper during the war, and one of the best. He was a good shot, but a good sniper required more than simple marksmanship to succeed. Slocum had the patience required to lie still and quiet for hours, waiting for the precise shot that would cause the most trouble for the enemy. The glint of sunlight off an officer's gold braid, the slow squeeze on the trigger, and the enemy floundered about in battle without a leader. He had been patient, he had been a good shot, and he had done more damage to the Federals than any dozen other soldiers in his unit.

"I am," he said simply. The two words carried more confidence than if he had launched into a detailed accounting of how he had learned marksmanship at his pa's knee and put it to use during the war.

"There is a bounty of ten dollars for every wolf hide you bring in," Frank Kincannon said. He impatiently motioned his brother to silence. "And last night I made the decision to double that. The other ranchers are putting up ten. I'll put up ten more for every hide.''

"The bounty's twenty dollars for a wolf?" Slocum wondered what trouble the ranchers were having. Usually a pack of wolves could be run to ground by a determined tracker backed by a dozen cowhands. When enough wolves were killed, the pack either disintegrated or moved on to less-dangerous terrain. Wolves were wily beasts. Self-preservation always drove them, sometimes more than with humans.

"It is," Kincannon said dourly.

Slocum glanced across the table at Elspeth. She dropped her eyes, then boldly locked her ebony eyes with his green ones. "Andy was killed by them.''

"Andy?" Slocum asked. Elspeth wasn't inclined to offer more. The answer came from William Kincannon.

"Our top hand," the girl's uncle said. "Wolves ripped him up something fierce. I tried tracking the wolf and couldn't.''

"So you reckon nobody can?" Slocum asked, edge in his voice. As much as he had taken a shine to Frank Kincannon, he had developed an immediate dislike for his brother.

"Something like that, Slocum," snapped William Kincannon. "Andy was a good man, and more are going to die because of the wolves.''

"Then it's about time somebody got to hunting them down. Back in Georgia I used to do a fair amount of hunting. I'd like permission to ride your spread and see what I can do." Slocum stared directly at Frank Kincannon, and wondered at the inner demons the man wrestled with. This shouldn't be a major decision. A killer wolf required a hunter to stop it. Kincannon obviously cared for his family and men and wanted to defend his herd from predators.

Why did he hesitate?

"That's a splendid idea, Papa," Elspeth said. Her mother started to speak, then bit her lip. Slocum saw the older woman didn't speak much, but from the way her eyes burned, a considerable amount of emotion boiled within her. "Will you hunt down this gray killer for us, Mr. Slocum?"

"Elspeth!" William Kincannon said, enraged for no good reason Slocum could tell. "You don't run the Sleepy K."

"And neither do you, Uncle Will. What about it, Papa?"

"I . . . I think you're right, dear," Frank Kincannon said.

The rest of breakfast was eaten in silence, the clicking of forks and knives against the plates the only sound in the room. Slocum had barely finished the thick steak and potatoes when Mrs. Kincannon took his plate and hurried off to the kitchen. William Kincannon excused himself and bustled after Mrs. Kincannon, his face a storm cloud of barely restrained anger.

"I reckon you want to get to the hunt right away, Mr. Slocum. Elspeth, go fix him some grub for the trail. If you need a rifle and ammunition, come on into the other room and choose."

Slocum followed Kincannon into a small room lined with racks holding shotguns, rifles, and six-shooters.

"I saw how the store in Bannock had stocked up on big-bore rifles. I've got a Winchester, which ought to serve me just fine, but I could use a few boxes of ammo."

"Help yourself," Kincannon said. He seemed unsure of what to say, then finally said, "These might not be the kind of wolves you're used to, Slocum."

"What kind might they be, Mr. Kincannon?" Slocum asked, not certain what the rancher meant.

"I've had some special ammunition made. You might

take this, just in case you need it.'' Kincannon opened a small drawer and pulled out an ammunition box. Almost reverently, with a slightly shaking hand, he opened the box and withdrew a silver bullet.

3

Slocum fingered the silver bullet Frank Kincannon had given him, then laughed at the notion it would be needed. He had spent enough time in New Orleans listening to folk stories to know about the superstitious French and their *loup-garou.*

"A wolf that changes into a man," Slocum said to himself as he mounted his horse. "The smelter fumes must have drifted out here and beclouded Kincannon's brain." He tucked the bullet away into his shirt pocket, where it pressed warmly into his chest. There was no call to believe anything unusual was happening on the Sleepy K, other than finding how many wolves ran with the pack that had killed the top hand.

Slocum had seen enough wolf kills to know how vicious wolves could be. A man, especially one wounded or frightened and on foot, didn't stand much chance against a determined, hungry pack. Wolves might prefer beeves or smaller animals, but a man was still prime pickings if they could bring him down fast.

Slocum headed due north from the ranch house, riding through a sparsely wooded area, and then turned down a valley when he saw fresh droppings that might have

come from a dog. Slocum dismounted and dropped to
one knee. The fresh dung pile might be the result of a
coyote, but Slocum didn't think so. Taking a stick, he
poked around in the tall grass where he had found it
until he pushed aside a thick clump and found a footprint
in the soft dirt.

"Too big for a full-grown coyote," Slocum decided.
He stood and looked up the valley, listening hard. Walking slowly, he found another, smaller paw print, then a
patch of blood and coyote fur. A slow smile of triumph
came to his lips. The wolf had surprised the coyote and
attacked it. From the torn-up ground Slocum recon-
structed the fight. The coyote might have gotten away,
but it was bleeding.

The wolf had been a big one from the size of its paw
print.

Slocum walked his horse, every sense alive. It was
getting toward noon, and most animals were safely hidden away for their daily siesta, but the day was cool in
the hills and he thought there might be some hunting
activity. The fresh blood and coyote fur told him the
fight had taken place less than an hour earlier.

"Breakfast," Slocum said, finding the ripped and
bloody coyote carcass. More than one wolf had feasted
on the carcass. Bloody tracks around the remains
showed how as many as a half-dozen wolves had fed
well on their kill.

Following the tracks of the wolf pack was easy. Slocum reached up and drew his Winchester from the
sheath, and then levered a round into the chamber.
He had the eerie feeling he was being watched. When
the sensation grew to the point where he wanted to
scream, Slocum tethered his horse where it could graze,
then went ahead on foot. The wind blew softly through
the stand of aspen, whispering and sighing, but it was a
snuffling noise that held his attention.

Hardly realizing he did so, he pulled the rifle stock to his shoulder and squeezed off a round. The bullet flew straight and true, catching the timber wolf just above the shoulder. A hair-raising, shrill screech sounded as air rushed from the dead wolf's lungs. It toppled to its side, kicked once, and then lay still.

"Twenty dollars," Slocum said to himself. He went to the animal and poked it with his toe, warily staying far enough away so he could put a second round through its skull if necessary. But his first shot had killed it cleanly.

He pulled out his thick-bladed knife, and had started to skin the wolf when the eerie feeling of being watched returned. Slocum looked around without being too obvious. If someone was spying on him, he wanted to find them before they realized he had spotted them. He saw nothing, but the area was curiously silent, as if all life had vanished.

Leaving his wolf for the moment, Slocum made a slow circuit of the small meadow where he had bagged the predator.

"Damn," he said when he stumbled over the body. Slocum stepped back, rifle pointed at the prone man. Then he knew there was no danger. The man was long dead, his throat ripped out by sharp fangs.

Slocum knelt and rummaged through the man's pockets the hunting for any hint about the dead man's identity. He found a pair of crumpled, sweat-soaked greenbacks and a leather pouch with a few shreds of cheap tobacco crammed into it. Otherwise, the man had ridden his last trail with empty pockets. From the look of his clothing he was a cowboy, probably one of Kincannon's hands.

Slocum's nose wrinkled at the fetid odor rising from the body. The cowboy had been dead for at least a day, maybe longer. It was cooler up here in the hills, and the corpse hadn't decayed as much as it might have at a lower altitude, where the summer still held the land in its heated grip. Slocum backed off, then turned back to the wolf he had shot.

"Are you the murderer?" Slocum asked the dead wolf. He hefted his knife and slit the animal from throat to rectum, letting its guts spill out. When the belly popped free of the body cavity, Slocum cut it open and examined the contents.

"You've chewed on something more than a man's throat," he decided. This might have been the wolf responsible for the cowboy's death, but he couldn't tell. The man had been dead for a day or more, but the contents of the wolf's belly were fresh. That didn't mean the wolf hadn't killed the cowboy, though.

Slocum finished skinning the wolf, and wound the pelt into a tight roll. He returned to fetch his horse, stowed the skin, and led the horse to the corpse. It took Slocum several minutes to lift the body over his saddle and secure it. Then he began the long walk back to Frank Kincannon's ranch house.

"First Andy, now Heck Larsen," grumbled William Kincannon. "I tell you, Frank, this is getting out of hand. Wolves are one thing, but you know what's really behind this—"

"Hush, Will," snapped Frank Kincannon. He glared at his younger brother. "It's complete nonsense. I don't want to hear another word about *that*."

Slocum kept a poker face as he listened to the argument. Something was going on between the men that he didn't understand. If he played fly on the wall long enough, he might find out what really troubled them. Whatever it was, it was more serious than wolves or dead ranch hands.

Both men turned and stared at Slocum. William Kincannon almost sneered, then spun and stalked off.

"We're all on edge, Mr. Slocum," Frank Kincannon said. "You did good."

"Twenty for the wolf hide?"

"I'll see to it. You want cash on the barrelhead, or you intending to go out and do some more hunting?"

"Hunt," Slocum said. "I came back early because of Larsen." He pointed in the direction of the body at the far end of the porch, a blanket tossed over the corpse.

"We'll see to a proper burial," Kincannon said. Been too many lately. "Too many."

Kincannon whirled around, hand going toward the six-gun thrust into his belt. He stopped when he saw his daughter in the doorway, looking pale and drawn.

"It's Heck, isn't it?" she asked in a small, choked voice.

"Wolf got him. Ripped his throat out," Kincannon said bitterly. Slocum wondered why he tormented his distraught daughter with such details. Slocum didn't think Elspeth was a hothouse flower, but there was no call for Kincannon baiting her the way he did.

Elspeth bit her lower lip and vanished without a word into the house. Kincannon went to the end of the porch and stood over Larsen's body, as if mounting an honor guard. Seeing there was nothing left for him here, Slocum mounted his horse and headed back into the hills.

He found the spot where he had discovered the body just as darkness slipped around, plunging the hills into deep shadow and making further travel dangerous. Slocum did a little scouting as he gathered wood for a fire. He tried to find out what had become of Larsen's horse, but found no trace of the animal.

Settling down, he ate a quick meal from the vittles Elspeth Kincannon had prepared for him that morning. Then Slocum lay back and stared up into the cloudless sky, picking out the patterns of constellations. His fire crackled gently a few feet away, warming him and slowly stealing away his consciousness.

Slocum awoke from his sleep with a start, reaching for his Colt Navy. He shoved it back into his holster and stretched a bit more to grab his rifle. He thought he heard someone laughing—and the laughter was answered by a wolf's mournful howl.

Coming to his feet, Slocum turned in a full circle to locate the wolf. The rattle of stones higher up the hill behind his camp betrayed the four-legged predator's position. Slocum dropped to a crouch and peered along a line parallel to the ground. When he saw the wolf's head outlined against the starlit sky, he fired.

A rattling animal death cry echoed down the hill, followed by a cascade of loose stones as the dead body slid downward. Slocum levered another round into the rifle chamber, then made his way uphill in the direction of the wolf he'd bagged.

He almost tripped over it in the dark. His shot had blown the top of the wolf's head clean off, killing it instantly. A grin came to his lips. He had been out less than a day and had made forty dollars. If he kept this up, he'd be rich inside of a week.

Then Slocum went cold inside at the sounds from uphill filtering down to his ears. More than one set of paws grated across the rocky ground. He backed down from the dead wolf and returned to his campsite. Kicking his fire to life with the toe of his boot, he peered into the night. Reaching down, he took a dry branch, got it blazing, and then sent it cartwheeling into the night.

He didn't see the wolves—not directly. A half-dozen pairs of shining silver eyes stared unblinkingly at him. He heard nothing but harsh breathing as the wolves ringed him and moved closer. Slocum stepped back, putting the campfire between him and the wolf pack.

Lifting his rifle, he fired in the direction of one pair

of eyes after another. He kept firing until the magazine came up empty. Slocum knelt, fumbled in his bedroll, and got out a box of cartridges. He reloaded quickly, trying to figure out how he was going to get out of here alive. The wolf pack had him surrounded.

Slocum fired into the dark, not hearing the shrill whine of a wounded wolf as reward for his marksmanship. He kicked more branches onto the fire, coaxing it higher and higher until he exhausted his store of firewood. But the knee-high flames were enough to send out a ring of light almost ten yards wide.

Crouching at the very limits of the light were the wolves. Slocum fired and shot another one, not killing it, but sending it howling into the night. The others became warier. Slocum tried to count the timber wolves, and couldn't. He emptied another full magazine and reloaded, letting the gray wolves creep closer.

He fired and wounded another. This seemed to take the fight out of the pack. They didn't realize his stack of wood had been exhausted. The wolves crept away, and then vanished into the night in search of easier prey.

Slocum heaved a sigh of relief, made sure his Winchester carried a full magazine again, then went hunting for more firewood. He built the fire until the heat on his face caused sweat to bead, then settled down on his bedroll, rifle across his lap, staring into the dark.

Slocum dozed and came awake a half-dozen times, always putting more wood onto the fire, until the first pink and gray fingers of dawn streaked across clouds to the east. Yawning and stretching mightily, Slocum got the kinks out of his tired muscles. He grabbed a piece of jerky and gnawed on it, then kicked out the fire and started on the trail of the wounded wolves.

At least two timber wolves carried his slugs. That was another forty dollars waiting for him. All he had to was track them down and finish the job he'd started the night before.

"All I have to do," Slocum grumbled to himself, knowing the danger of tracking a wounded predator. He had been lucky the night before, and knew it. Now it was time to make sure such a situation never occurred again. The wolf pack might have turned on its wounded members, but he couldn't count on it. Slocum had no idea how badly injured either of the wolves he had hit might be.

He swept across the edge of the meadow in a wide arc until he found droplets of blood. He started on the trail, the spoor obvious. Paw prints appeared every now and then in the soft earth, before disappearing across a rocky patch. He had little trouble following the wounded animals, though, because of the blood trail they left. He didn't have to be a bloodhound to follow this track.

An hour into the hunt, Slocum stopped and looked around, alert. He cocked his head to one side, and heard faint ghostly laughter far ahead. It rose until it reached a hysterical pitch, then died abruptly. It might have come from the same throat that produced the laughter he'd heard before, but Slocum could not tell for certain.

"What the hell is that?" he wondered aloud, then returned to the trail. He reached the edge of a stand of pines, then froze when he heard a deep-throated snarl. With a smooth movement, he lifted the rifle to his shoulder, aimed, and fired. The bullet blew splinters and sap from a pine tree and sent the gray timber wolf running clumsily.

Slocum took off after it and overtook it quickly. The wounded wolf spun about, snarling and gnashing its teeth. Slocum's bullet from the night before had caught it in the hindquarters, causing the beast to limp.

His second shot killed it cleanly.

A new howl of pain and anger rose from the far side of the stand of pines.

"The second wolf," Slocum decided. He reached into his pocket and replaced the rounds he had used on the dead wolf at his feet. Having a full magazine gave him a more secure feeling. He had found the wounded wolves but not the rest of the pack.

Slocum skirted the wooded area, and came up on the wolf from the flank. This gray wolf had been more severely injured than its pack mate. Slocum's slug had broken its front leg.

"Not bad for shooting blind," Slocum decided. He had spoken softly, but the wolf had heard him and twisted around. Another bullet from his rifle whistled toward the wolf—and missed. The wolf hobbled off into the undergrowth.

Slocum cursed under his breath and set off in pursuit. When he reached the spot where the wolf had crouched, he heard the taunting laughter again. Slocum spun around, trying to pinpoint the source.

"Who's there?" he shouted.

The laughter began to fade—in the direction taken by the wolf. Slocum headed into the brush, more determined than ever to bag the wolf. He picked up the pace, seeing spots of blood here and there. The bushes had been broken and trampled by the fleeing wolf, making the track obvious to a blind man.

Slocum stopped at the edge of a rocky stretch. A few drops of blood hinted at the direction taken by the wolf. Slowing his pace, every sense vigilant, he crossed the stone-strewn hillside until he came to the far side, where soft earth began again.

Slocum blinked in disbelief, looked around, then stared at the footprints.

Footprints, not paw prints. On the far side where Slocum had started, a wolf had crossed the stone field. In front of him, where the wolf ought to have exited, were footprints. Small, bare human footprints.

4

"Can't tell you more than I have," Slocum said, eyeing Frank Kincannon's foreman closely. Quinton Barnsley had taken an inordinate interest in Slocum's story of tracking the wounded wolf across the rocky patch, only to find human footprints on the far side. Most men would have laughed at Slocum, or thought he was pulling their leg.

"The size of the footprints," urged Barnsley. The tall man made nervous gestures, playing with his beard and stroking over his bushy nut-colored mustache constantly. "Big, little, a man or a woman? You gotta have some idea who made 'em, Slocum."

"Small. Might have been a large boy's prints."

This didn't satisfy the foreman. He tugged on his beard some more, then asked, "Could it have been a woman's foot you saw?"

"Reckon so," Slocum said, frowning slightly. "I heard a shrill laugh before I found the tracks. That might have been a woman laughing hysterically. But I didn't see another living soul out there. Just the wolf pack."

Barnsley scratched his head and squinted nearsightedly. He spun about as if he'd been scalded when his

31

boss came from the ranch house and jumped down from the end of the porch. Kincannon looked peaked, as if he had been up long, sleepless hours. More than that, he looked as if he'd been the one Slocum had been hunting. He had a trapped-animal appearance that made Slocum wonder if Kincannon might lash out unexpectedly.

"Counted your hides. You're doing good work, Slocum. Six of them, all with clean bullet holes in them. You look real close at the carcasses?"

"No closer than I have to," Slocum said, wondering at the question.

"You, uh, you have to use that special bullet I gave you?"

Slocum touched his shirt pocket. The silver bullet still rode easy there.

"Regular lead works just fine on these timber wolves," he said. This seemed to provide a moment of relief for the rancher. The moment passed, and he again took on the harried expression.

"I'm having some problem with the wolves going after my cattle," he said. "Quint can give you details. You want to follow the herd a while and see if you can't bring down a few more of those gray killers?"

Slocum shrugged. He didn't care where he shot the wolves. Tracking them was dangerous work, and sometimes difficult. Wolves were cunning creatures, and knew every trick imaginable to throw even the best tracker off their scent. Slocum had found solitary wolves rather than ones running with the big pack after his first encounters—the ones where he had found Heck Larsen and the strange human footprints.

Trailing the herd and waiting for the pack might give him a chance to bag even more in relative comfort. He could eat chuck with the cowboys and find what their thoughts were on the wolves, on their boss, on strange happenings around Bannock. Slocum glanced at Barnsley, and wondered at the man's insistent questioning. Something more than hungry wolves bedeviled the Sleepy K.

"Good," Kincannon said, showing a curious combination of relief and consternation. "Quint, show him where the herd is. You stay out there and—"

"But Mr. Kincannon, you need me here to watch af—"

"Show him," Kincannon said sharply. A flicker of fear flashed in the rancher's eyes. Then Kincannon stormed off.

"What chores you have around here that a regular hand can't do?" asked Slocum.

"Forget it." Barnsley glanced in the direction of the front door of the ranch house, nodded brusquely, and followed his boss. Slocum hesitated when he saw Elspeth Kincannon coming out of the house.

"Mr. Slocum, you're back. I heard Papa say there were more wolf hides."

"I've shot ten so far," Slocum said. The count pleased him, and he hoped it would impress Elspeth. She was about as pretty a woman as he could remember seeing. It took him a second or two to decide how she looked different from when he'd first met her. Elspeth had been tanned, a clue to the amount of time she spent out in the sun. Now she seemed paler, as if she had not left the ranch house for more than a few minutes in the past week.

"You must be a fantastically good hunter," she said.

"I do what I can," Slocum said. Before he could say anything more to her, Barnsley bellowed at him to saddle up and ride. "Have to go."

"See you again soon, I trust, Mr. Slocum." Elspeth waved at him almost shyly, but there was nothing shy in the brazen light in her dark eyes.

Slocum touched the brim of his hat and went to follow

Barnsley. The foreman had already trotted from the yard and headed up a steep hill to the west of the ranch house. It took Slocum the better part of fifteen minutes to catch up.

"What's the rush?" he asked Barnsley. The foreman shot him a glare that might have fried eggs.

"Don't go gettin' too friendly with Miss Elspeth," Barnsley said.

"You sweet on her?" Slocum asked.

"No," was all the foreman said. Slocum didn't press the obviously touchy matter. They rode in silence the better part of the afternoon, finally arriving on the rim of a broad, grassy bowl in the mountains. Slocum shielded his eyes from the sun and looked out at the herd. Scattered around the valley, the herd might top one thousand head. It was far larger than Slocum would have guessed.

"They're sitting ducks if the wolves get into the valley," Slocum said. "You might think on bunching the cattle up some more."

"Hard to do right now, shorthanded like we are," Barnsley said. His earlier anger seemed to have passed, and he concentrated solely on the plight of the beeves. "The outriders do what they can to bring in the strays."

"You're going to have to winter them soon enough, or round them up and get them to market," Slocum said. "Why not start now and keep them from the wolves?"

"That's up to Mr. Kincannon," Barnsley said. He started tugging at his beard again, betraying how nervous he was about the subject.

"The place where I bagged most of my kills was in that direction," Slocum said, pointing to the northeast. "Any easy way into the valley from that direction?"

"Several," Barnsley said. "That's the problem. There's no natural barrier to those damned gray killers."

"I'll grab some chow and then go scout out some

likely spots,'' Slocum said. ''I can sit and wait to see if the pack comes in, or maybe just a single wolf.''

Slocum perked up when he saw a cowboy down in the valley waving a blue bandanna to attract their attention. Slocum and the foreman rode down quickly to the young man, who was all flustered and red in the face.

''Quint, them wolves,'' the man gasped out. ''They got a half-dozen head last night. No matter how me and the rest of the boys tried, we couldn't stop them.''

''You looked frazzled from lack of sleep,'' Slocum said.

''We all stayed up to keep the wolves at bay. Didn't do a bucket of spit's good. And all day we been tryin' to bring in the stragglers.''

''Get some sleep,'' Barnsley said. ''Slocum here's a wolf hunter. He'll help out tonight. There's no way you can do double duty like that and not fall out of the saddle from exhaustion. I'll stick around a day or two and help out.''

''Thanks, Quint. We just don't know what to do.''

The hint of hysteria in the words alerted Slocum to still another bad situation on the Sleepy K. He kept his mouth shut and his eyes and ears open as he ate a quick meal. Conversation ebbed and flowed around him, giving him a sense of the frustration and anger the cowboys felt at the wolf pack for its unceasing predation. But even more interesting was the way Quinton Barnsley turned defensive whenever Kincannon was mentioned. It was as if the foreman hid a terrible secret.

''Getting on to dusk,'' Slocum said, heaving himself to his feet. He checked his rifle and made sure his saddlebags were filled with spare ammo. He didn't want to be ringed in by the wolves again without enough firepower to turn back any possible attack.

''You want me to send a couple of the boys with you, Slocum?'' Barnsley said it in such a way that it meant he was being polite, that he really wanted to keep his hands close to the herd.

"I'll take care of it. Don't want to shoot anyone by accident. Hunting wolves is hard enough," Slocum said, swinging into the saddle. He rode to the northeast, figuring this might be his best chance at picking off any of the timber wolves sneaking into the valley.

Before he reached the rim, a wind whipped down from the heights, carrying a hint of rain with it. He peered at the sky and saw thunderheads building. Lightning began stabbing out in the darkness, but it was so far away Slocum paid it no mind. He couldn't even hear the thunder.

Finding a game trail, he settled down, rifle resting in the crook of his left arm. He sat with his back to a tree amid a fragrant patch of clover. This might go a ways toward hiding his scent from the wolves' ever-sensitive noses. Slocum had half nodded off to sleep when scratching sounds alerted him to the presence of an animal. He jerked awake and brought his rifle around, pointed up the game trail.

Eyes gleamed at the top of the rise.

Slocum fired, and was rewarded with a mocking bark. He had missed the wolf. Scrambling to his feet, he rushed up the trail. When he reached the spot where the wolf had stood, he saw nothing in any direction.

"Damnation," he said, knowing he had spooked the timber wolf and driven it away. The wolf would wait a spell, then find another path into the valley.

Deciding to move closer to the edge of the Sleepy K herd, in case the wolf pack had already slipped past him, Slocum rode slowly through the dark, picking his way carefully to keep his horse from stepping into an unseen gopher hole.

The cry of human pain caused Slocum to throw caution to the wind. He put his spurs to his horse's flanks and shot into the darkness, galloping straight for where the Sleepy K herd lowed away in the night.

More screeches of pain caused Slocum to wheel about and dismount in a hurry. He ran to the dark, writhing heap in the middle of the meadow. He laid down his rifle and rolled the man over.

"Barnsley!"

"Slocum, man tried to kill me. Cut at me with a knife. Hurt me bad."

"Don't talk," Slocum cautioned. He picked up his rifle and scouted around the area, growing more puzzled by the minute. He saw only Barnsley's tracks mingled with a few cattle—and a lot of wolf tracks. He listened for the distinctive howl of a triumphant wolf, and heard nothing but the cattle growing increasingly restive. On foot, with a herd working itself up into a fright, Slocum knew his and Barnsley's future might be pretty grim.

He returned to the foreman and dragged him up and across his shoulders. Slocum staggered a little under the weight. The bearded man appeared slender, but his loose-fitting clothes hid considerable bulk.

"I'll get you back to the ranch house and patch you up," Slocum said. "First we have to skedaddle out of here. I don't cotton to the notion of those cattle stampeding."

"Wasn't a wolf," Barnsley said weakly. "Human. It was human. Naked human . . ." His words trailed off as he passed out from the pain.

"What happened?" came the frightened question from an outrider. The youngster trotted over and saw his foreman slung across the saddle in front of Slocum.

"Barnsley's hurt bad. Somebody needs to keep the herd quiet. The beeves are thinking hard about stampeding."

"In the dark?" The youth shuddered. "I'll tell Billy.

He's acting foreman when we're out here without Quint.''

"I'll get Barnsley back to the ranch house."

"He looks like he's hurt bad enough to need Doc Talbot from town."

"I'll see what Mr. Kincannon has to say about it. His wife or daughter might be able to patch up Barnsley just fine." Slocum knew different, unless one of the women had the skill of a trained doctor. Barnsley was bleeding like a stuck pig and needed considerable attention. Slocum thought about leaving the foreman at the camp and riding for help, then decided this was best. It would take twice as long getting help for the foreman if he left him here.

If the herd stampeded, nowhere in the valley might be as safe as dangling over Slocum's saddle on the way back to the Sleepy K.

Slocum's horse tired quickly under the double weight, forcing Slocum to dismount and walk alongside. The pace set this way through the night was slow but sure, interrupted only by distant thunder and Barnsley's occasional moans of distress. That told Slocum the man was tough and still alive. Otherwise, the foreman didn't even twitch until they returned to the ranch house a few minutes before dawn.

"Mr. Kincannon!" Slocum called as he walked his horse up to the front of the house. "Barnsley's been hurt!"

Slocum expected the Sleepy K's owner to come out. Instead Elspeth rushed out, her face paler than ever and her expression one of horror.

"What happened?" she asked. "Papa and Uncle Will are out. They went to fix the fence along the road last night."

"You or your ma have any skill patching up a wounded man?"

"What did that?" Elspeth looked even more faint, but she didn't avert her eyes when she saw the full extent of Barnsley's injury. "It looks as if something tried to rip his throat out."

"Missed by inches and got his chest," Slocum said.

"A wolf?"

"He said it was a man."

"What? Why would anyone do this to him? One of our cowboys?"

"If you or your mother can't help, I think I'd better get a wagon hitched up and drive Barnsley into town. One of the hands said there was a good doctor there."

"Dr. Talbot," Elspeth said. "Yes, he's a good man, very qualified."

She ran off. Slocum didn't know where, and didn't have time to ask. He laid Barnsley on the front porch and told him, "I'll get you into town before you know it." He looked up, and saw Elspeth had fetched Barnsley some water. She carefully dripped it onto his dried lips. The man seemed strong in spite of the blood loss. From what Slocum could make out on the man's chest, he had been slashed three or four times—deep—with a knife.

Or was it a wolf's claws that had done the damage? The equal spacing and the injury done looked more like the work of an animal than any human wielding a knife.

Slocum rushed to the barn and got the wagon hitched up. He threw straw into the back and grabbed a few blankets to make the trip easier for the foreman. He hitched up a team and drove back to the front of the house. Elspeth had continued to care for Barnsley, tending him with water and trying to make him rest more easily.

"I'll help," the lovely young woman offered, giving Slocum a hand in moving Barnsley from the porch into the wagon bed.

"Much obliged. I'll be back when I can," Slocum said.

"That's all right," Elspeth said, jumping into the wagon. "I'll ride along and do what I can for Quint. He's about the best foreman we ever had. At least, he's about the only one who ever got along with both Papa and Uncle Will."

"You shouldn't go," Slocum said. "What if your pa comes back and finds you gone?"

"Mama will let him know, if she can remember," Elspeth said almost bitterly. "Now come along. Every second counts. The man is seriously injured, after all."

Slocum knew better than to argue. He heard determination in Elspeth's voice. Never quarrel with the boss's daughter, especially when she can prove useful along the road into Bannock.

Slocum gee-hawed and snapped the reins and got the team pulling. They were used to a lighter load, and almost galloped from the yard. He slowed their pace, and kept them moving on the less-rocky parts of the road to ease the burden on Barnsley.

About halfway into town, Elspeth climbed onto the hard seat beside him. "I think he's sleeping," she said. "Either that or he has passed out. Whatever it is, he isn't in any pain right now."

She sat with her hands folded primly in her lap.

"Thanks for helping out like this," Slocum said. "Sometimes the daughter of the boss thinks such comforting is beneath her station."

"I'd *always* help," Elspeth said indignantly.

"Don't know you well enough. And it was a compliment," Slocum said.

"No offense taken," she said. They rode along for another hundred yards in silence. Then Elspeth said, "John—may I call you John?—what is happening?"

"I don't understand."

"They are keeping something from me. What is it?"

"Who is?" Slocum was as much in the dark as Elspeth Kincannon about the strange undercurrents flowing back and forth on the Sleepy K.

"Papa, Uncle Will, even Quint. It has something to do with the wolves, but there is more, and I don't know what it can be."

"I just shoot wolves," Slocum said. He had heard the fear and apprehension in the men's voices too, but he didn't know what that meant.

"You're more than a hunter. I can tell. You think all the time. I can see how you appraise people, weigh them, and come to decisions. What do you think of me?"

The question took him by surprise. Before he could answer, a bolt of lightning lashed down and blew apart an oak tree beside the road. He fought hard to keep the team from bolting.

". . . close," he finally heard Elspeth say. Her lips moved some more, and then she clamped them shut. For a moment, she said nothing. Then she laughed. "Can you hear again?" she asked.

"Barely. Thunder deafened me."

"Me too. John, we'd better hurry. I don't like the look of the storm."

Rain fell in heavy gelid drops now. He urged the horses to greater speed, but in the increasingly muddy road it became too hazardous to pull fast. He edged to the side of the road and bounced and rocked along the shoulder. Slocum went from worry about Quinton Barnsley reaching town alive for the doctor to work on, to simply getting there in one piece himself.

The heavy rain turned into a frog-strangler, cutting off vision entirely. Slocum couldn't see beyond the team, but blindly traveled on. They had to get the foreman to the doctor—and shelter.

5

"Where's the road?" called Elspeth, her voice faint in the roar caused by the driving rain.

Slocum had no answer. He kept the horses moving, hoping the wagon wouldn't get bogged down. Elspeth had covered Quinton Barnsley with a tarpaulin, but the man had to be worse off than ever by now. The noise of the rain hammering on the tarp over his head would be deafening. Just off the brim of Slocum's broad-brimmed hat, the sound drowned out everything else in the world.

The wagon slewed to one side and threatened to mire down in the mud, but Slocum found a rocky patch that provided a moment of purchase. The wagon lurched ahead, and then found a deep mud hole that sucked in the wheels to the hub. The precarious cant to the wagon told Slocum it would take more effort than he was able to expend to get them free.

"We got to get on into town on foot," he shouted.

"How far, John? I can't see a thing?"

"Maybe you ought to stay with Barnsley," he suggested. Then he knew that would never do. How could he ever find Elspeth and the wagon again in this hard-driving rain? He and the woman had to leave Barnsley. Carrying the wounded man would doom them all.

"We can ride on the horses," Elspeth said, her lips pressed close to his ear. "Put Quint over one and then . . ." Her voice trailed off as the wind whipped a sheet of rain away and revealed a building.

"We're already in town," Slocum said, amazed. The downpour had been so hard he had not seen any hint of Bannock. From his memory of the town, they were actually halfway in, not far from the saloon where he had been hoodwinked.

"Dr. Talbot's office, John. There!" Elspeth pointed through the rain. Slocum wasted no time slinging the wounded foreman over his shoulder and staggering through the storm. Elspeth opened the door and helped him inside.

An elderly man, more bald than gray-haired, peered up over the tops of his spectacles. He dropped the book he was reading onto the desk and exclaimed, "Close the damn door! You're gonna flood the whole blessed place!"

Slocum dropped Barnsley onto an examining table, and let the doctor rip away the bandages Slocum had put on the foreman. Talbot took a half step back when he recognized Barnsley. The doctor sucked in a deep breath, licked his lips, and then rubbed his hands together in a peculiar nervous gesture.

"Damnation, he's been cut up something fierce. How he lasted this long is a damned miracle, dammit if it isn't."

"Will he live?" asked Elspeth.

"How the hell should I know? Quint's a tough son of a bitch—no offense, Miss Elspeth. If anyone can make it, he's the one. Now get on out of here and let me get to work. This is going to get damned messy. Damned messy, yes." Talbot licked his lips again, then wiped his hands on the sides of his baggy trousers.

Slocum started to ask the doctor where he expected them to go in the storm, but Elspeth silenced him. She pulled him toward the door.

"We can get a room at the hotel," she said in a low voice. "Dr. Talbot is a strange duck, but a good surgeon. It's best to do as he says."

"You get the rooms, I'll see to the horses," Slocum said. "I don't reckon there is anything I can do for Barnsley that I haven't already done."

"Hurry, John. There's only the one hotel we can reach without getting lost in that sea of mud. The Grand Emporium just across the street."

"I want to get dry," he agreed. They ducked their heads and braved the full force of the rainstorm. If anything, it had gotten worse. Slocum watched Elspeth vanish into the teeth of the storm. He worked hard to calm the horses and led them down the street until he found the livery. Inside, it was warm and fragrant and dry. He almost hated leaving, but Elspeth was expecting him.

Slocum dashed from one overhang to another in a vain attempt to keep out of the rain. All this tactic afforded him was some sense where he was in Bannock. If anything, he got wetter dawdling than simply putting his head down and running.

He popped into the hotel lobby, water draining off him in rivers. Slocum shook himself like a wet dog, not caring if he got the rug and walls wet. Going to the desk clerk, he started to ask for his room. The man shoved a key toward him, paying little attention.

"Thanks," Slocum said sarcastically. He climbed the narrow flight of stairs to the second floor. Here and there along the walls ran rivulets from the leaky roof. It was still better than being outside. Slocum checked his key and found the right room. He thrust it into the lock and turned.

As he stepped into the room, he sensed someone already inside. His hand went to his Colt Navy, then paused.

"I thought you'd never get here," Elspeth said from under the covers in the bed.

"I'm sorry. The clerk gave me the key, and I thought this was my room."

"It is," she said, sitting up and letting the covers drop. Slocum stared at her bare breasts, white mounds of slightly bobbing flesh that mesmerized him.

He sat on the edge of the bed. Elspeth moved closer, the covers falling from her. She was stark naked as she waited for him.

"Are you sure you want to do this?" Slocum asked.

"We don't have any choice," Elspeth said, a wicked grin on her lips. "There was only the one room left, our clothes are wet, there's only one bed, what else can we do?"

Before Slocum could answer, she kissed him hard. It took him only a second to respond. She melted into his arms, warm and alluring. He had thought she was a fine-looking woman from the instant he had set eyes on her. That she was as attracted to him as he was to her came as something of a surprise to Slocum. Elspeth had seemed bold enough, but directed in other ways.

His hands moved down her sleek body, cupping her warm breasts. She pressed closer to him, crushing them into his palms. Somehow her hands worked on his clothing, pulling off his shirt and unfastening his gunbelt and letting it fall to the floor amid a pile of her wet clothes.

Slocum twisted and turned and stripped off his boots and jeans, and crawled under the covers with her. A thrill of excitement passed through him as he felt her naked body moving against the full length of his. She lifted one leg and clamped her thighs on his upper thigh.

Then Elspeth began rocking back and forth, cooing like a dove.

"So nice. You feel so nice," she said.

He kissed her lips and eyes, and worked to one shell-like ear. He nibbled at her earlobe as his hands roved her willing body. She arched her back and crushed herself into his muscular frame.

"You're so strong." She kissed his chest and belly, and avidly worked lower. Slocum gasped when her lips found his manhood. Her tongue whirled about, and left behind tiny dots of saliva. Then she worked her way back up his body, kissing and licking as she went.

Slocum wrapped his arms around her and rolled over. Her legs parted as he moved into the vee that they formed. His spit-dampened tip brushed across the fleecy nest hidden between her legs.

"Yes, John, yes. I want you now. Now, oh!"

Elspeth arched her back and lifted her buttocks off the bed as he slipped into her. Slocum echoed that gasp. He was surrounded by hot, moist female flesh that crushed down powerfully on him. For a moment he remained hidden away in Elspeth's most intimate recess. Then he pulled out.

She moaned softly, then began clawing at his back and crying, "Do it now, now, John. Hard. Take me like an animal in rut!"

He moved faster this time, sinking full-length into her. Her clawing left bloody scratches on his back, spurring him to stroke even faster. He fell into the age-old rhythm of a man loving a woman, then could stand no more. She sapped his strength and stole his iron control. His hips flew faster and faster, and heat built up that spread throughout his body.

Elspeth gasped and shrieked like a wild animal. She tensed and clung powerfully to him as Slocum spilled his seed.

They continued moving in unison until Slocum was unable to continue. He sank down, his arms still around her. The lovemaking had gone fast. For such a genteel lady, Elspeth had intense desires.

"That was a good start," she said, snuggling into the circle of his arms. "How long before you're ready again?"

"Again?" Slocum asked.

"See?" Elspeth said, stroking over his flaccid organ. "There's life there now. It might take a few minutes."

"A few minutes?"

"With help," she said, diving back down under the covers. Slocum surprised himself and delighted them both by responding so quickly to her oral ministrations. They made love again, slower, more languidly, as the rain hammered against the tiny window and the bed creaked in gentle protest to their movements.

The sun turned Bannock into a steam bath. Slocum wiped sweat from his face as he put his shoulder to the wagon wheel and pushed hard. It took several tries before he and the three men helping him got the wagon rolling.

"Surely did mire down," the clerk from the mercantile said. "You going to get back to the Sleepy K all right if you take on a load?" He looked over his shoulder toward his store. It was apparent he figured Slocum would patronize his store in exchange for the effort he'd expended.

"Won't need too much," Slocum said. "I need a few bags of flour and . . ."

"And two bolts of cloth, Mr. Naylor," said Elspeth, coming along the boardwalk, picking her way carefully to avoid the boards that had broken or been washed out.

"Figure your pa might also need some ammunition," Slocum said. "I can get that at the general store."

"Go on, John," Elspeth said. "I want to see if Mr. Naylor has anything more than the cloth that would be suitable for a project I have in mind." She smiled, and made Slocum worry that she might be thinking of a wedding dress. They had gotten along better than he had thought they would. But the insatiable gleam in her eye seemed more than simple physical lust to him. He wasn't sure he was ready for more than they had done already.

Still, most men would jump at the chance of marrying a filly like Elspeth Kincannon. She was spirited and pretty, and her father owned a good-sized ranch.

Slocum touched the brim of his hat and headed for the general store, passing the Quick Buck Saloon. Men turned brown from mud stood along the bar, sipping at beer and knocking back shots of whiskey to dispel some of the aches and pains earned by digging out from under the mud that had inundated Bannock.

He would have passed on, but a man with a strong Cajun accent stood on a chair at the back of the saloon and bellowed, "This is cure for what ails you all. I guarantee it. I have only just come to this here town, but I see the problem. You are beset by a menace I know all too well, being from Baton Rouge in the fine state of Louisiana. They sneak about, but we know the cure."

He reached into a bag and pulled out a silver bullet. He thrust it high above his head so it caught the faint rays from the gaslight high overhead. In spite of himself, Slocum reached up and touched his pocket, his fingers tracing the outline of the silver bullet Frank Kincannon had given him.

"They are the *loup-garou,*" the man said in a lower voice that caught everyone's attention. "They are not human, oh, no. And they are not wolves. They are both—and neither."

"What you goin' on about, Frenchie?" growled one burly miner.

"I am telling you of ancient lore, of stories told only by one Acadian to another. I share this because I care for you, *mon ami*. I will share the secret of my people, the way to kill *loup-garou*."

"A bullet'll blow the brains outta any wolf," the miner growled.

Slocum sidled into the saloon, pressing his back against the outer wall. He had no desire for a beer or whiskey, but he wanted to hear more of the Cajun's spiel. Slocum had seen too many patent-medicine peddlers, but none with such appeal. The entire crowd gave the Cajun their rapt attention.

And he knew why. The ranchers had lost their beeves—and cowhands—to wolves. Slocum had heard the all-too-human laughter, followed wolf tracks that turned into human footprints . . . and Quinton Barnsley had claimed a man had attacked him when the only tracks around him were cattle hooves and wolf paw prints.

"Not *any* wolf, oh, no," the Cajun said in a conspiratorial whisper that brought the crowd closer to hear. "*Loup-garou* can change from man to wolf and back, just like that!" He snapped his fingers. The sound caused many in the crowd to jump, as if they had been poked with a needle. "And *loup-garou* cannot be killed by a regular bullet. You need a special one, you do."

"Like what?" Slocum called, knowing the answer before the man spoke.

"Silver is their curse. A silver bullet will rob them of their ability to change from man to wolf and back. A silver bullet like this one will *kill* the *loup-garou*!"

"I shot one of them gray devils," muttered a man near Slocum. "Hit him dead-on, and it never slowed. Never could track it down either."

"I heard that!" cried the Cajun. "A silver bullet would have stolen away its vile life 'fore it took yours!"

Slocum turned when he heard heavy footfalls coming along the boardwalk. A man burst into the saloon, wild-eyed and out of breath. Gasping for air, he managed to get out, "Lem's done been attacked. Wolf. Edge of town!"

Slocum recoiled. Wolves were cunning beasts and seldom came near a town. They probably didn't like the human stench—or the number of rifles, shotguns, and six-shooters that could be brought to bear on them.

"Who's Lem?" he asked the man next to him.

"Town idiot. Got hit in the head by a falling timber up at the Silver Deuce mine a couple years back. Never right since then."

"Are you sure it was a wolf?" Slocum asked.

"Doc Talbot's workin' on poor ole Lem right now. Said it's the second worst he's ever seen. Only Barnsley from out at the Sleepy K was worse."

Slocum tried not to appear too surprised, but he was. Talbot had examined Barnsley and decided it was a wolf that had attacked the Sleepy K foreman. Yet Barnsley had claimed a human had cut him with a knife. Slocum had never seen such evenly spaced knife slashes before, but that didn't mean it wasn't possible. One thing that bothered him about a man attacking Barnsley was the need to slash three times to leave such a wound. A wolf needed only to swipe at a man once—and Barnsley was a strong opponent for either a human or a *loup-garou*.

Slocum shook himself. He was buying into the Cajun's wild story of a wolf that changed into human shape.

"Gimme two of them fancy silver bullets," called a miner. "I'm not lettin' any *loup-garou* gnaw on me the way they did on Lem!"

This set off a rush to buy the Cajun's silver bullets. The man in front of Slocum bought six at ten dollars a cartridge. From all Slocum could tell, the bullets weren't silver, but had only been painted to look that way. Even if the men who ought to know minerals noticed this, they said nothing.

The Cajun wasn't selling real silver bullets; he was peddling hope and a feeling of security. The wolves were running roughshod over the town. This gave the men a way to fight back.

6

"Good to see you moving around," Slocum said to Quinton Barnsley. The Sleepy K foreman moved slowly and painfully, but he was walking on his own. He sank heavily into the back of the wagon, half lying across a bag of flour.

"You saved my bacon, Slocum. Thanks."

"Wasn't the only one," Slocum said, indicating Elspeth Kincannon. She was still dickering with the owner of the mercantile over the price of several bolts of cloth. Two lay in the back of the wagon, but she wanted more. Slocum wondered what she needed so much for.

"Miss Elspeth's a peach," Barnsley said. Slocum heard the admiration and something more in the foreman's voice.

"We need to get back to the Sleepy K," Slocum said. "I need to tell Mr. Kincannon about the wolf attack outside of town. The wolves are getting bolder."

"Lem," Barnsley said. "He died while Doc Talbot was working on him." The foreman shuddered. "I saw what those sons of bitches did to him. Ripped him apart." As he remembered, Barnsley touched the wounds on his own chest.

53

"You sure it was a man who did that to you?" Slocum couldn't get the idea out of his mind that all he'd found were cattle and wolf tracks around Barnsley. Unless someone had carefully followed Barnsley, stepping into the man's boot prints, some human track would have been left.

"I—" Barnsley bit his lower lip and averted his eyes. Slocum knew whatever else the man said would be a lie. "Don't remember. Must have been loss of blood that done it to my memory."

"John, Quint," Elspeth said brightly. "I see you're both ready to return to the ranch. Good."

She allowed Slocum to help her into the wagon, where she settled down on the hard bench seat beside him. As soon as Slocum got the wagon rattling along, trying to miss the muddier patches in the road, Elspeth spoke.

"Did you hear anything about the Wellington ranch being sold?"

"Wellington?" Slocum had heard the name, but couldn't remember where.

"You mean old Josh sold his spread?" said Barnsley. "His pa died on that land. I can't believe he'd up and sell. Unless . . ."

"Unless what?" asked Slocum. He saw both Elspeth and Barnsley were upset over something.

"Mr. Wellington lost his only son to the wolf pack," Elspeth said. "Brutal death, from the sound of it."

"He's right protective of his three daughters," Barnsley said. "They're young, and he'd turn tail and run before letting anything happen to them."

"He could send them back East," Slocum said.

"He wouldn't do that," Elspeth said. "I heard rumors he'd sold his ranch for only a thousand dollars."

"A thousand!" cried Barnsley, who winced at his overly exuberant outcry. "It's worth fifty times that."

"I know," Elspeth said. "The strange thing is that no one knows who bought the spread. And Mr. Wellington has already left."

"Where's Wellington's family hail from?"

"Somewhere down south. Louisiana, I think," Elspeth said. "He always hung strange little wreaths on his door, claiming they brought good luck."

"Or held bad luck at bay," Slocum said. He had been in New Orleans and seen the *gris-gris* superstitious people hung on their doors to turn aside voodoo curses. He wondered if the Cajun selling the silver bullets in the saloon had had anything to do with the purchase of the Wellington ranch. Then he had his hands full trying to keep the team out of a muddy bog along the side of the road. In a day or two, the sun would dry the dirt out enough to afford purchase, but that was a couple days away. All the way back to the Sleepy K, Slocum struggled with the team and heavily loaded wagon.

Slocum rode slowly back into the yard stretching in front of the Sleepy K ranch house, wondering what the furor was. A dozen houses were tethered out near the barn, and men sat on the front porch. Cora Kincannon moved among them, giving each a glass of lemonade. Slocum turned and made sure his skins were still securely tied to his saddle. This week-long trip had seen him cut down eight more of the wolves. But the more he killed, the more seemed to run. He didn't understand it.

"Mr. Slocum, come on up and join us. Lemonade?" invited Frank Kincannon.

"Sounds mighty good to me," Slocum said. He dismounted, and saw how the men stared at the pile of skins. It wasn't until he saw a battered tin star pinned on one man's chest that he tensed up a mite. He had too many wanted posters offering rewards for his capture not to get uneasy at the sight of a lawman and this many deputies.

"This is Marshal Jenks. Don't reckon you two have met before."

"Been out killing wolves," Slocum said, shaking the lawman's hand. He was glad to see that Jenks paid him even less attention than the deputy back in Bannock. Something worried the man more than the possibility of running across a fugitive from a judge-killing charge in Calhoun County, Georgia.

"The marshal and his posse have been out hunting two-legged wolves," Kincannon said. Slocum said nothing, knowing the lawman would tell him what the purpose of this excursion might be.

"Prisoners over in the penitentiary," Jenks said. He scratched at a nit, and then twirled the ends of his seedy mustache as he spoke. "At least five got clean away. We're out huntin' for 'em. You see any trace of men on the run, Slocum?"

"Just wolves," Slocum said. "I found a small pack trying to cut out a heifer up in the northeast pasture. I got lucky and bagged several, then tracked the others, but I never saw hide nor hair of any men."

Slocum wondered at the way Frank Kincannon stiffened at this. It was as if he had touched a hot branding iron to the man's hindquarters.

"I'm lookin' for a man who knows Mr. Kincannon's rangeland," Jenks said. "You willin' to join up so we can hunt them killers down?"

"That's up to Mr. Kincannon," Slocum said.

"Go on, Slocum. You're trading shooting four-legged killers for two-legged ones." Kincannon was uneasy as he spoke.

"From the last trace we got of them, they might be heading due south," Jenks said. "If we cut straight to the east, we might get between them and Utah. Any problem with that, Slocum?''

"Should there be?'' Slocum shrugged. He turned when he heard Quinton Barnsley come up, four cowhands trailing behind, obviously reluctant to go on what might be a wild-goose chase.

"Got some more men for your posse, Marshal,'' Barnsley said. ''We're ready to ride.''

"Quint knows the territory better than I do,'' Slocum said, angling to get out of being deputized.

"You're the best damned shot I ever saw, Slocum,'' said Barnsley. ''You'll be needed when we run those bastards down.''

"What'd they do?'' Slocum asked.

Barnsley answered, ''The five of them held up the bank in town. Killed two folks, a little girl and her ma. They're bad ones, Slocum, real bad ones.''

"Let's ride,'' Slocum said, seeing he had no way to back out now. He pulled down the eight skins and dropped them on the porch. He looked up to see Cora Kincannon watching him the way a snake watches a bird. Tipping his hat politely, he wasn't too surprised when she spun on her heel and left without saying a word.

He hoped to get a glimpse of Elspeth, but the young lady was nowhere to be seen. Slocum settled into his saddle again, tired from being on the trail for a week and knowing he might be out for another.

Barnsley rode up beside him, riding knee to knee. For a few seconds the foreman said nothing. Then he spoke.

"Thanks for coming along, Slocum. This means a lot to me. That was my sister and niece what got killed in the robbery.''

"Sorry to hear that,'' Slocum said, meaning it. The frontier was a hard place to live, but unarmed women and children stood no chance against armed bank robbers.

"I know the place where they have to go if they want to get south without going near Bannock," Barnsley said, eagerness coming to his voice now. "We'll get between them and freedom. Don't know if they're armed, but none of them's likely to get away if I have a say in it."

They rode the rest of the morning. When the posse stopped to eat lunch, Slocum scouted ahead. The lay of the land was pretty much as Barnsley had said. Slocum wondered if this section of land butted up against the Wellington spread. From his notion of where Kincannon's land stretched, it might be they'd ridden off the Sleepy K and onto the ranch so recently sold.

His rumination on property ownership faded when he caught sight of a man stripped to his waist darting in and out of low bushes down by a meandering stream. The man wore black-and-white striped prison trousers. Slocum gentled his horse to keep it from betraying him. The escaped prisoner hadn't spotted him.

A dozen different tactics flashed through Slocum's mind. He might ride back and get the posse. They weren't more than twenty minutes away. Or he could take on the prisoner himself. The man seemed to be alone, but four others had to be out there somewhere. One escapee Slocum could handle, but five?

The situation changed even as he considered fetching the posse. The prisoner spotted him and lit out running. Slocum put his spurs to his tired horse's flanks in an attempt to overtake the man. He changed his mind when the convict spun about, fumbled, and pointed a sixshooter in his direction.

Slocum didn't wait for the convict to get off a shot. He whipped up his rifle, steadied himself as his horse galloped along, then squeezed off a round. Slocum wasn't sure who was more surprised, him or the convict, when the bullet caught the man squarely in the chest. The escapee stood up straight, his six-gun dangling from lifeless fingers. He took a half step forward and collapsed bonelessly, dead before he hit the ground.

Reining back, Slocum came to a halt beside the dead man. From his position on horseback, he scanned the area for movement. This had to flush out the other prisoners.

He saw a white flash across the meadow as someone ducked into a stand of live oak. Twisting around, Slocum saw Barnsley riding up. The Sleepy K foreman had to be trailing him to get here this fast. But then came the marshal and the rest of the posse. Their lunch break had been shortened for some reason. Slocum raised his rifle and pointed in the direction of the corpse.

Marshal Jenks reached him, panting from the hard ride.

"You got one, good. That's two down."

"Two? You found another one?" Slocum didn't see any prisoner among the posse, and he had not heard a gunshot. As far as he could tell, none of the posse had been left behind to guard a prisoner.

"Dead," Barnsley said. "Throat ripped out by a wolf. We found the body not a dozen yards from where we camped to chow down."

"Two dead," Slocum said, "three to go. And I know one's over there."

Marshal Jenks had already sent men from the posse to flank the small thicket in an attempt to cut off escape. He lifted his arm like a cavalry officer preparing for a charge, then dropped it in the direction of the woods.

Slocum hung back, not eager to kill anyone else. From the look of pure hatred in Barnsley's eyes, more blood would be spilled. The posse galloped forward. Slocum wondered how heavily armed the convicts might be. The one he had shot had waved around a six-gun, probably stolen from a prison guard during the breakout.

"Barnsley, Slocum, ride with me," Marshal Jenks called out. "The rest of you, split into groups no smaller than three. Start through the woods and flush them sonsabitches out!"

Slocum realized the marshal was a smarter man than he appeared at first blush. Jenks knew Barnsley was on a manhunt with the intent of killing all the gang that had murdered his sister and niece. This way, both Slocum and the marshal could watch out for Barnsley.

Slocum's concern for the foreman ran a bit deeper than his need for revenge. It had been only a week since Barnsley had been savaged, and he wasn't entirely up to full strength yet. Barnsley's will might get him into a tight spot his body wouldn't get him out of.

They rode slowly, ducking low-hanging limbs. Now and then Slocum stopped and listened hard. He was sure he had seen the convict enter the woods. It might be possible the man had gone to ground, daring them to find him rather than trying to outpace his pursuers. But Slocum didn't think so. The escapees had had flight in mind when they'd taken off, and they would keep running.

If they knew anything about the first convict who had fallen prey to wolves, they would keep moving no matter how smart it might be to lie low until the posse swept past.

"Slocum, hear that?" asked Jenks. The marshal tipped his head to one side, looking straight ahead into the woods.

It took Slocum a few seconds. Then he heard the crackling of bushes as something heavy moved through them.

"Barnsley, wait," Slocum cautioned. "The one I cut down was armed. This one might be too."

"He'll get away!" protested the Sleepy K foreman.

"Not from this posse," Jenks assured him. "I want them alive, if we can."

"How'd they escape the noose?" asked Slocum. Bannock must be a more law-abiding town than he thought if a lynch mob hadn't formed after the five were caught.

"One of them's pa is lieutenant governor. He's fighting to get his boy free. The others are going along for the ride."

"Not two of them," Slocum said. "Let me go ahead on foot and see if I can flush him."

"You might serve the cause better laying back. You're the best shot in the posse," Barnsley said. "Let me go on in. You back me up. I trust you with my life, John."

The foreman's earnest plea pushed Slocum in the direction of a bad mistake. Letting Quinton Barnsley go after the convict meant nothing but trouble. The marshal settled the matter for them.

"You two hang back. I'll go get him. That's what the town pays me the twenty dollars a month for, after all." Jenks dropped from the saddle and drew his rifle from its scabbard. He took a deep breath, glanced from Barnsley to Slocum, then set off.

"Go over there. Get to the side so you can get a clear line of fire," Slocum told Barnsley, sending the man to the south as he drifted north. If Jenks ran into trouble, both of them had to be able to fire freely without risking hitting the lawman in the back.

Getting edgy at the marshal's slow progress, Barnsley began creeping up to the undergrowth where they had heard the noise. Slocum realized it might be nothing more than a jackrabbit, but he didn't think so. The sound had been made by a larger animal—a man-sized animal.

The sudden quiet in the forest caused Slocum to react. Birds stopped singing, and even the wind died down.

Shots rang out, bullets ripping through the leaves above his head. He let out a rebel yell and charged, firing his rifle as he went. Jenks crashed through the thornbushes and fell heavily. On the other flank, Barnsley emptied his six-shooter, and then fumbled to get his Winchester pulled from its sheath so he could keep up the barrage.

"There, Slocum, there he is!" shouted Barnsley.

Slocum saw not one but two men dodging through the trees, heading north. He fired twice, but missed both. The outrageous shot that had killed the convict in the meadow had exhausted his luck for the day. He had to slow his horse's headlong attack to keep from being whacked in the head by low-hanging limbs.

"The posse will nab them," Slocum called to the marshal and Barnsley. "Let 'em go!"

"Yeah, let them go," Jenks said. "Take a look at this, Slocum."

Slocum dismounted and let his horse rest from the galloping. He walked slowly to where the marshal had stumbled and fallen. Only when he was on top of the lawman did he see that Jenks had not tripped over a fallen tree trunk.

"Jehoshaphat," Barnsley said, eyes wide. "Another of them fell to the gray devils."

"Looks like it," Jenks said. "Throat's ripped out, just like the other one we found. The wolves are doing a better job bringing them to justice than any of us, except Slocum."

Slocum moved closer and stared down at the escaped prisoner. The man lay curled up as if he had tried to protect himself, but Slocum saw the wounds on the man's destroyed throat.

The marshal was right about how the man had died. He just wasn't correct about the killer. Slocum had seen too many wolf bites not to recognize one instantly. This man's throat had been ripped out by teeth residing in a human mouth.

7

"You're right handy rounding up strays, Slocum,"
Frank Kincannon said, the compliment sounding more
rote than real. The owner of the Sleepy K had a distant
look in his eye, as if his body was here and his mind
was a hundred miles off. "Thanks for helping out, especially since it doesn't pay near as well as killing
wolves."

Slocum had shot three more wolves, claiming the
bounty on them. Since he had started hunting the gray
predators, he had earned almost three hundred dollars.
His work with the Sleepy K hands had come about almost as a spare job when several cowboys simply
packed their gear and left one night. The discontent
among the remaining cowboys was obvious—and Slocum was a mite surprised that Quinton Barnsley was the
man doing his best to foment it.

"I do what I can, but you need at least five more
hands if you want to get the beeves moved before winter," Slocum said.

"Winter?" Kincannon had drifted away again, as he
did often now when talking to his men. Slocum followed
the man's line of sight to Elspeth's bedroom window.

He hadn't seen the lovely woman in several days.

Fact was, he had not seen her since Marshal Jenks and the posse had tracked down the escaped prisoners from the penitentiary. The story told by the pair of convicts who had bolted from the forest still sent shivers up and down Slocum's spine.

They told of a shaggy man—or maybe a manlike creature—chewing away at the throat of their friend. The marshal's charge into the underbrush had spooked them even more, driving them into the guns of the men Jenks had sent to flank the woods.

But their frightened stories were almost incoherent except when it came to the description of the beast. It wasn't a wolf. And it wasn't a man.

Loup-garou, Barnsley had said loud and often after hearing this. He and the Cajun selling the silver-painted bullets in Bannock had struck up a real friendship, and the foreman took every chance to rattle on about the dangers stalking the Sleepy K.

"Might better spend my time going after the wolves," Slocum now said. "Can't say I've reduced the pack much, but they can't keep coming after men without paying for it. I've never seen such numbers and such determination in a wolf."

"Wolf? What did you say, Slocum?" Kincannon swung back, tearing his attention from his daughter's window.

"I haven't seen Miss Elspeth lately. Is she sick?"

"She's fine." The sudden flare of anger was far and away out of character for Frank Kincannon. "Why do you ask?"

"Haven't seen her in a while," Slocum repeated. "Didn't mean to pry."

"Then don't," Kincannon said sharply, stalking off toward the barn. As he went, Slocum considered following the cowboys who had already left the Sleepy K. All that held him to the ranch and working for a man who treated his men in such a fashion was Elspeth Kincannon.

Slocum wondered if she had taken ill. Or if it was something more. Something worse. That would explain Kincannon's fierce denial.

He considered going to the house and asking for her, now that Kincannon had gone into the barn, but decided against it when Barnsley rode up.

"Slocum, get your horse. We got to round up some of the heifers down by the river. A couple got bogged down."

"Wouldn't want them breaking any legs," Slocum agreed. He mounted and rode beside Barnsley, thinking about Kincannon and Elspeth. When Barnsley spoke, it pulled him out of his reverie.

"Werewolves, Slocum, that's another name for them. Pierre said so."

"That the Cajun selling the silver bullets?"

"He's a knowledgeable man. Don't mock him." Barnsley's lips thinned to a determined line as if he would defend Pierre's honor unto death.

"You been going into Bannock a lot lately. Is it only to hear what that rabble-rouser has to say?"

"What else would it be?" Barnsley's sudden defensiveness reminded Slocum of how Frank Kincannon had acted when he'd inquired after Elspeth. A simple question produced a response far out of balance. "Are you accusing me of something?" Barnsley demanded.

"Just making an observation."

"You think on this, Slocum. There's going to be a wolf one of these days you can't kill with that rifle and ordinary ammunition of yours. You'll need one of these!" Barnsley grabbed his six-shooter and rolled out the cylinder, showing Slocum that all the bullets were the silver-painted ones sold by the Cajun.

"There's a cow mired down," Slocum said, ignoring the silver-painted bullets. Riding high in his shirt pocket was the silver bullet Frank Kincannon had given him before he had begun hunting wolves. But how had Kincannon come to the conclusion back then that a silver bullet might be needed?

Too many questions went galloping without answers. Slocum pulled his lariat free and roped the remnants of the cow's horns, letting Barnsley do the messy work of slogging through the mud to get a rope under the cow and around its hindquarters. Together, they pulled the cow free. It snorted angrily and swiped at them with its horns, then walked off, as unconcerned as if it hadn't been close to death.

Somehow, Slocum found it incongruous. The cow didn't care that it had been stuck, or much consider that they had freed it. And everyone at the Sleepy K seemed to worry about—what?

"Who do you think this *loup-garou* really is?" Slocum asked suddenly. Barnsley sat up in the saddle as if he had been stuck with a pin. His face drained of blood under its leathery tan, and his hand shook slightly.

"What's that mean?"

"You're the one, you and the Cajun, who say there are men who turn into wolves. That means we ought to be rubbing elbows with them when they're not all furry and howling at the moon."

For an instant, Slocum thought Barnsley was going to draw his six-gun again and shoot him. Then the foreman took his hand away from the butt of his six-shooter. If looks could kill, Slocum guessed he would have died then and there.

"You're makin' fun of me, Slocum. I don't like that."

"With so many men leaving the Sleepy K, there are fewer choices for the culprit," Slocum pointed out. "I'm not making fun of you, just asking an obvious question.''

"I've worked for Mr. Kincannon for well nigh twelve years, Slocum. I'm loyal through and through. Don't ever think I'm not. He and Miss Elspeth treat me like one of the family.''

"And Mrs. Kincannon?''

"I'd die for them," Barnsley said, thrusting his jaw out belligerently. The more innocent questions Slocum asked, the madder the foreman became.

"Never said you were anything but true blue," Slocum said, trying to soothe the foreman's ruffled feathers. Barnsley was mighty nervy for no reason Slocum could tell. Finding that reason began to take on an urgency for Slocum. He had the feeling of standing on the railroad tracks, watching a freight engine steaming down on him.

They finished pulling another cow from the mud not a hundred yards down the stream. Then Barnsley curtly dismissed Slocum as if he were an annoyance rather than an experienced cowboy. Slocum said nothing, returning to the ranch house. He had a worry, and thought he ought to bring it to Kincannon's attention.

Slocum thought everything over on the way back to the house. No matter how he turned it over in his head, the undercurrents around the Sleepy K tugged at everyone. The image of the trapped cattle kept coming to him. They were all mired down, waiting for the river to rise and drown them.

He rode to the barn, where Kincannon still worked like a common cowhand. He was pitching straw into the stalls for the horses, his face set in a grim mask. Slocum had seen men working on their demons. Kincannon was doing that now.

"Mr. Kincannon, I need to talk with you about Barnsley.''

"What's wrong? Quint feeling poorly? I've worried

over him not being recovered from his . . . wounds.''

Again Kincannon seemed incapable of speaking without strange lapses. He turned distant before Slocum even put his concerns into words.

''Barnsley's been agitating among the hands,'' Slocum said, choosing what he said carefully. ''He's spreading rumors that a *loup-garou*—what he calls a werewolf—is preying on the cattle, and maybe the men who've been killed.''

''Do you think that's true, Slocum?''

''Haven't seen anything that I can't explain.'' Even as Slocum said this, he knew he lied. Barnsley had been attacked in the middle of a meadow, only hoofprints and wolf tracks around him. Yet he had claimed a man had slashed him. And the convicts had insisted their friend had been killed by a wolf-man. They had been more frightened of the beast than of returning to the penitentiary, where they might eventually get their necks stretched for murder.

''Quint has quite an imagination,'' Kincannon said. ''I don't think he believes it is any more than a good story to tell around the campfire.''

''He's spooking your men. That's why you've lost as many as you have in the past few days. If Barnsley keeps his jaw flapping, you're going to be working the Sleepy K all by yourself.''

''He doesn't have a mean bone in his body,'' Kincannon said. ''You don't know him. If you want to ride on, Slocum, do it. We managed before you rode up. We can manage without you.''

''I'm not quitting. There are still plenty of wolves out there,'' Slocum said. ''If the bounty stays on their heads.''

''I . . .'' Kincannon opened his mouth, then snapped it shut. He finally said, ''I've been thinking about it. The threat from the wolves is declining. Might not be necessary to keep a bounty on them.''

"I've never seen wolves as stubborn when it comes to attacking men," Slocum said. "Barnsley and Lem in town, the two convicts, and the boy over on the Wellington spread."

"Poor Isaac," Kincannon muttered. "And Zeke Claremont's boy was attacked two nights back."

"The owner of the spread to the west of the Sleepy K?"

"He's selling out and moving on."

Slocum said nothing. Wellington had sold out too, for similar reasons. Someone was buying up land cheaply because of fear of the wolves. Now Kincannon wanted to stop the bounty because he wanted the threat to be over.

"Well, Slocum," said Kincannon in a firmer voice, "thank you for telling me this. I have every confidence in Quinton Barnsley and know he would never do anything to harm either the Kincannon family or the Sleepy K."

Slocum knew he would get nothing more from the rancher. He stopped outside the barn, his gaze fixed on Elspeth's window. If the woman was ill, he ought to pay his respects. If it was something more, Slocum wanted to find out. His curiosity bump was starting to ache. If her father wouldn't level with him, maybe Elspeth would share the truth with him.

He walked toward the house, wondering how he would get past Cora Kincannon. The woman had shown no friendliness, and had gone out of her way to let him know, without coming right out and saying it, that she wished he would ride on. Slocum doubted Mrs. Kincannon would let him see her daughter, with or without a proper chaperon.

As he went up the front steps, he heard movement

inside the house. The door stood ajar. Slocum peered through, and saw Cora Kincannon going into the kitchen. Rather than risk her refusal, he slipped inside and walked on cat's feet to Elspeth's bedroom. He rapped lightly. From inside the room came a weak moan.

Slocum opened the door and felt as if someone had punched him the belly. Elspeth lay on her bed, white as a sheet and thrashing about as if she fought unseen ghosts. He closed the door behind him and sat on the edge of her bed. The woman's hand was clammy and her pulse raced, causing a blue vein on the side of her slender neck to protrude rhythmically.

Slocum laid his hand on her head. She moaned and opened her eyes. He had seen fever victims who were in better shape.

"What's wrong?" she asked. "Why are you here?"

"I worried about you. Your pa wouldn't tell me what happened to you."

"I . . . I started having fainting spells," Elspeth said in a weak voice. "Dizzy. I bumped into things." She held out her arms, showing bruises on the forearms and extending up into the sleeves of her dressing gown. "And there were the nightmares. Terrible ones filled with blood and people dying . . . and me. I was always there."

"With dying men?"

"Yes," she said, her voice taking on a note of panic as she remembered her nightmares. "It was as if I caused their deaths." A trembly hand went to her mouth. "I don't feel good, John. My stomach is upset."

"What have you eaten?"

"I can't remember. Nothing."

"For days?"

"I don't know." Elspeth sat up in bed, looking stronger now. Tiny dots of color returned to her pale cheeks. She threw her arms around him and held him close. "I ought to know. I can't remember. How long have I been in my room? It's light outside."

"You've been here for almost a week," Slocum said. "That's why I started worrying." He pressed his hand against her forehead again, checking for fever. Her skin had a curious texture to it, like old leather and yet damp.

"It doesn't seem that long, yet it does. Oh, John, the nightmares!" She burrowed her pallid face into his shoulder. He felt hot tears on his shirt. Slocum held her, more curious than ever about what was going on at the Sleepy K.

"Here, take a drink," Slocum said, handing her a water glass from the table beside the bed. She sipped at it and made a face.

"Bitter," she said, then drained the glass and smiled wanly. "I was thirstier than I thought."

"You might consider going for a ride, getting out of this stuffy room," Slocum said. "Anytime you want, I'll ride with you. We can go into town or just ride around the yard." He doubted either her parents or Quinton Barnsley would approve of that, but Slocum wanted Elspeth out in the fresh air where she could again bloom. In this hothouse, she was fading away like an old daguerreotype.

"Quint's been getting my medicine for me, so I don't need to go to Bannock," she said. The unfocused look in her eyes told Slocum she was losing hold on the world. She sank back to the bed, again white as a fluffy summer cloud. Her eyelids fluttered, and then she drifted off to sleep, a small incongruous smile on her lips.

What thoughts went through her mind? Slocum could not guess. He stood and went to the bedroom door. Opening it a fraction, he scouted the hallway. Slocum saw Cora Kincannon come from the kitchen, wiping her hands on a towel. She tossed it aside and came bustling down the hall toward her daughter's bedroom. Slocum slipped behind the door and waited for the woman to come in. Instead, the click-click of her shoes passed the door and went toward the rear of the house.

Slocum peeked through the opening again, and saw Cora Kincannon leave the house through the back door. She stopped just outside, giving Slocum the chance to leave through the front, but as he stepped into the hall, he heard a gruff voice out back.

He could have left, but he needed to find answers to a few of the questions plaguing him—and bearing on Elspeth.

He went toward the rear, and stopped where he could look out and see Mrs. Kincannon talking with her brother-in-law. William Kincannon spoke rapidly, in a voice so low Slocum couldn't hear. Cora Kincannon moved closer to him and laid a hand on his arm.

William Kincannon took her in his arms and held her close. Slocum started to leave, thinking they were sharing troubling news, possibly about Elspeth and her condition. Before he turned, he saw Cora lift her head and kiss William Kincannon.

The kiss was more than friendly. It was hard and passionate and squarely on the man's lips. And Frank Kincannon's brother did not back off from his sister-in-law as she pressed her body into his. His passion matched hers as she lifted a leg and curled it around his waist. She began rocking up and down, his thigh between her legs.

Slocum wondered what else he might see if he kept spying on them. Ending up with more questions when he had expected to discover explanations, he tiptoed down the hallway and out the front door to his tethered horse. A nightlong wolf hunt might give him time to think and get his thoughts into order.

Slocum was wrong. He found neither wolf nor verity that night.

8

The hunt had not gone well for John Slocum. He had spent four days tracking wolves, but had failed to see so much as a single hair on a timber wolf's head. Three hundred dollars rested in his pocket from earlier kills, but he came up empty this time, which indicated that maybe the wolf pack had finally moved on.

That made sense to Slocum. He had never seen wolves as tenacious as the ones bedeviling Bannock. And he had certainly never heard of a wolf pack staying around, no matter how bad the conditions in their usual territory, when men started hunting them down.

"Wolves with a taste for human flesh," Slocum said, shaking his head in disbelief at such a notion. Wild animals usually avoided men and their towns. "Even if they didn't actually eat their victims, they've killed a passel of men."

Something in this reflection made him frown, and sent his thoughts running down strange passages. The wolves had killed but had not devoured their victims, except possibly for the first cowboy he had found dead. Slocum had to admit it might not have been a wolf responsible for devouring the man. Coyotes and buzzards and other scavengers could have worked on the man as easily as a wolf.

But there were so many men and boys in the area killed by wolves.

This set him thinking about Elspeth, and the ranches surrounding the Sleepy K, and how men were packing up their families—or what remained of them—and moving on because of the wolf attacks. He rode back toward the ranch house, wondering if it was time for him to drift on. He had never intended to stay this long, but Slocum felt some duty toward Elspeth. Never in all his travels had he seen a woman go from the very picture of health to pale, drawn, and frail in such a short time. Her once-sharp mind seemed foggy with nightmare, and for no discernible reason.

That uncertainty bothered Slocum the most. It was another question for which he had no answer. The more the questions built up, the more determined he became to find the explanations.

As he topped a rise that led to the road from Bannock, Slocum reined back and waited a few minutes. A rider on the road galloped along, hell-bent for leather. Slocum wondered who was in such a powerful hurry. He got even more curious when he recognized Quinton Barnsley. The Sleepy K foreman rode with his head down, using his spurs and lashing with the ends of his reins.

Slocum wondered if something had gone wrong at the ranch, then came to a decision. There was nothing he could do at the ranch if there was something seriously wrong with Elspeth. He might be able to help in Bannock, however. Getting Doc Talbot out might require more persuasion than Barnsley could muster. Or so Slocum told himself. He headed down the steep hill and came out on the road.

He looked toward the Sleepy K, then turned his mount and trotted in the direction of Bannock. Barnsley would kill his horse if he kept up the furious gait. That meant he would have to slow eventually or be on foot. Slocum maintained a steadier, slower rate, and arrived in town only a few minutes after the foreman.

Slocum almost called out to Barnsley when the man rode past Dr. Talbot's office. Slocum dropped to the ground and went into the doctor's surgery. Talbot sat behind his desk, running his finger down the side of the newspaper. He peered at Slocum, heaved a sigh, then said, "Who've you brought me this time, Slocum?"

"No one. I thought I saw Quinton Barnsley come in here," he lied.

"He get himself cut up again?"

"He's mended all right?"

Talbot scowled. "Damn right he has. I fixed the son of a buck up. When they walk out of here, they don't fall down dead. Damn me!"

"Any more wolf bites?" Slocum saw the sudden slyness cross Talbot's face; then it vanished. He might have only imagined it. Slocum knew he was exhausted from futile hunting and long days in the saddle.

"None in the past few days. I think the wolf pack has moved on. About damn time, I'd say. If there's nothin' you need, get the hell out of here and let me work."

Slocum smiled crookedly. Work consisted of reading the Salt Lake City *Desert News*. That was fine with Slocum. It meant the doctor wasn't needed for more serious pursuits.

Slocum left and walked slowly down the street, spotting Barnsley's horse outside a saloon. Poking his head inside confirmed what he had suspected. Barnsley knocked back one shot of whiskey after another, as if he was trying to erase an unpleasant memory. After three quick shots, the Sleepy K foreman slammed the shot glass down and loudly proclaimed, "One more. Then I got to move on."

"Sure thing, Quint," said the barkeep. He poured another shot, then waved off the man's money. "On the house. We appreciate all you and Mr. Kincannon have done for the town. You're staying when everyone else is hightailin' it."

"Heard how Zeke sold out," Barnsley said, slurring his words slightly. The liquor had gone straight to his brain. "Think a couple other ranchers are selling too. Know Wellington's gone back to Louisiana."

"I heard," the barkeep said.

"Thanks," Barnsley said, turning and almost falling over his own feet. Slocum spun around and dropped into a chair just outside the saloon door. Pulling his hat down to shield his face, he waited for Barnsley to stagger past.

Barnsley muttered to himself, "Damn shame. Shouldn't happen. Not like this."

Slocum had no idea what the foreman meant. He pushed up the brim of his hat and watched as Barnsley weaved across the street and went into the town apothecary. Standing, Slocum started to cross the street and see what went on inside the pharmacy, but Barnsley came boiling out, no less sober but more determined now. He carried under his arm a small package wrapped in brown paper.

As he had ridden into town, so did Quinton Barnsley leave Bannock. At a full gallop.

Slocum decided he could find out more following Barnsley. The pharmacy wasn't going anywhere. At least, not as fast as the Sleepy K foreman. Barnsley took off at a clip that would wear out his horse within a mile. Again, Slocum was kinder to his mount, but he knew he could never overtake the man. He cut across country, riding through a section of fence that had fallen into disrepair.

The Wellington spread. Abandoned, but sold to someone. And the Claremont ranch. Slocum wondered how difficult it would be to find out who had bought such a large expanse of land for a mere thousand dollars. Fear did things to a man, especially when his family was threatened.

Cutting through a valley and urging his horse up a steep, grassy slope brought Slocum to a rise not a half mile from the Kincannon ranch house. He guessed he had beaten Barnsley back, but by how much he couldn't be sure. Shielding his eyes with the pulled-down brim of his dusty Stetson showed Slocum the tranquil picture of a Montana spread. Peeling back the thin skin of that calm revealed a rot Slocum could not understand—not yet.

He saw a pale Elspeth come out onto the porch, only to be caught by her mother when she seemed to sag. Cora Kincannon swung her daughter around and pushed her in the direction of the front door. This got Slocum moving, letting his horse pick its way down the steep hill by itself. He wanted to be certain nothing happened to the increasingly sickly woman. She seemed to get continuous care, but Slocum had the gut feeling Elspeth was in trouble *because* of that care.

He wished he could put the inchoate thought into words, but couldn't. Still, he had gotten through the war trusting his instincts. When others had died for no good reason, he'd survived because of his sense of "rightness" and "wrongness."

Instead of going straight to the house, Slocum dismounted, left his horse a hundred yards away, and approached on foot. He was wary of running into William Kincannon. The sight of Frank Kincannon's brother and wife kissing as they had put Slocum on edge. This was one more thorn burrowing its way into his hide. Trouble was brewing, and he ought to be riding away from it instead of bulling his way into it.

But he couldn't avoid trouble because of Elspeth. He

felt he owed her something more than ignoring the trouble swirling about her trim ankles.

The sound of hooves against the ground sent Slocum diving for cover. Barnsley came riding up on an exhausted horse barely able to stand. The foreman jumped off, patted the horse and murmured something to it, then climbed the four steps to the front porch. Before he reached the door, Cora Kincannon came bustling out.

Slocum couldn't hear what they said because of a brisk wind whipping from his back toward the house and swallowing the words. He crept closer, until he worried about being seen due to lack of cover. He found a spot where he could watch, if not hear, and settled down to see what went on between Barnsley and his boss's wife. Slocum didn't think there would be the affection she had shown her brother-in-law.

And there wasn't.

The foreman handed her the small package brought from the pharmacy. Cora Kincannon snatched it from the man's grip and clutched it to her breast. Then she stamped her foot and angrily berated Barnsley.

Slocum took the opportunity to move closer, finding some small concealment behind a haystack. He might have edged ten yards closer, but the wind picked up and spun their words away even more than before. Not daring to move again, Slocum simply spied on them, wondering at the bone of contention between them.

"No!" he heard Barnsley shout.

Mrs. Kincannon said something in a lower voice, but her reply carried with it the lash of command. Barnsley stepped back and shook his head before pointing toward the barn. Cora Kincannon grabbed his arm and pulled him in the opposite direction.

"He ought to know. This is important!" Barnsley shouted again.

Mrs. Kincannon fingered the small parcel, shook her

head, then turned and left Barnsley alone on the porch. Barnsley continued to yell after her, but to no avail. He heaved a deep sigh, rubbed his mouth with the back of his hand as if hankering for a drink, then grabbed the reins on his horse and headed for the bunkhouse.

"No balm in Gilead, not on the Sleepy K," Slocum said to himself, wishing he could have overheard the argument. He quietly returned to fetch his horse, circled, and rode slowly into the barnyard from a different direction.

Slocum waited for the foreman to mention his trip to town or the parcel he had brought for Mrs. Kincannon. But if anything, Quinton Barnsley was more taciturn than ever, burning inside and cold outside. After evening chuck, Barnsley flopped down in a chair in the bunk-house and stared at a blank wall.

Slocum started to strike up a conversation with the foreman, then bit back his words when Barnsley stood suddenly and said, "I'm going to look for those lost yearlings."

"Want company?" Slocum asked.

"I can do it myself. Let me alone, Slocum." On the way out, Barnsley slammed the bunkhouse door so hard, several of the drowsing cowboys sat bolt upright, hands going for their six-shooters. They looked around, saw nothing, and lay back down, snoring in seconds.

Biding his time, Slocum considered tracking Barnsley. In the dark it would be hard, and chances were good the foreman would see him. Slocum could always claim to be out hunting wolves, that their paths had just happened to cross, but Barnsley would never buy that. He'd been a decent enough gent when Slocum had first ridden up to the Sleepy K. In the intervening weeks, the foreman had become jumpy and downright spiteful.

Slocum reckoned it had something to do with the

package Barnsley had fetched for Cora Kincannon. He sighed heavily as he lay back on his bunk. The easy thing for him to do was ask the pharmacist what the Sleepy K foreman bought.

Thinking over the problems, Slocum drifted to sleep, only to be awakened a little after midnight by the sound of a galloping horse.

"Who's comin' that fast?" muttered a young cowboy from the next bunk. "Damn-fool thing to do. Horse could step in a gopher hole in the dark." The cowboy rolled over and tugged at his blanket.

Slocum rose and went to the window facing the ranch house. Seeing William Kincannon almost fall from his lathered horse, Slocum grabbed his gunbelt, strapped it on, and was outside in the wink of an eye.

"Frank, Frank!" called William Kincannon. "Get your ass out here. There's been trouble, bad trouble!"

"What happened?" Slocum asked. William Kincannon glanced at Slocum, started to speak, then turned when his brother boiled out of the ranch house, a shotgun clutched in his shaking hands.

"It's Quint. I found him. God, Frank, it was awful!"

Slocum watched the play of emotion across Frank Kincannon's face. The rancher looked from his brother to over his shoulder, as if he wanted to duck back inside his house. The pull was powerful, but Frank Kincannon resisted.

"Slocum, go find out if Barnsley's all right," he ordered.

"Where'd you leave him?" Slocum asked William Kincannon. The man wasn't as frightened or agitated as he made out. A glint of calculation shone in his eyes as he described the path he had taken back to the house and how he had found Quinton Barnsley.

"What condition's he likely to be in?" Slocum asked. Will Kincannon shook his head and made funny gasping sounds. Then he got out, "He's dead, Slocum. No man could be wounded like that and not be. I panicked when I saw him. He . . . no one should die like that!"

"I'll see what I can find out," Slocum said.

"Come into the house, Will," called Cora Kincannon. The woman held the door open for her brother-in-law. Slocum wondered if Frank saw the interplay between the pair. He doubted it, because he would have missed it himself had he not seen Cora and Frank kissing as they had.

Slocum saddled and rode slowly along the dark trail toward the north. It meandered around, but Slocum stuck to it, not sure how far he had to ride before coming upon Barnsley's body. Even though he was taking it easy, the sight of the foreman's carcass came up on him fast.

His horse reared, and Slocum fought to control it. Then he dismounted and examined the body. He had seen men blown apart during the war. Minie balls did terrible things to a man's flesh and bone, but the sight of Barnsley's ripped-out throat sickened him. Holding down his gorge, he used a stick to push away the blood-soaked shirt and reveal fully Barnsley's throat.

It had been savagely slashed. If Barnsley had died instantly, it would have been a favor. From the expression of stark terror permanently etched on the dead man's face, Barnsley had not died easily—or fast.

Slocum tossed down the stick and made a slow circuit of the area. Part of the ground was strangely free of any spoor. Slocum located bootprints that probably belonged to William Kincannon. But another set of small footprints—not a wolf's paw prints—caught his eye. Slocum reached down and measured the print with his hand.

"Large barefoot boy," he said. "Or a small woman." Slocum sucked in a deep breath, almost gagged from the smell rising from the body, then backed off. On foot he followed the footprints leading from the scene. All the while he kept alert for any hint of wolf tracks. He didn't find them.

It almost lay beyond his wildest nightmare that a human could have attacked Barnsley in such a ferocious manner.

Dropping to one knee, Slocum pushed away low grasses and found a complete footprint. Looking up, Slocum saw a ghostly white mist floating between trees not twenty yards away. A soft moaning rode on the gentle breeze. His hand went to his six-shooter and drew it before he advanced.

Shrill giggles alerted him before he swung around the tree, Colt Navy leveled and cocked. It took all his willpower to keep from squeezing the trigger, but he was glad he had not fired first and asked questions later.

Elspeth Kincannon was directly in his sights. The wind tugged at her nightgown and pressed it against her slender body. She stared at him, a vacant look on her face. She drooled—and caused more blood to drip down the front of her already blood-soaked nightgown.

9

Slocum took Elspeth by the shoulders, guided her toward a nearby tree stump, and gently pushed her down. She stared at him with her flat, lifeless ebony eyes, as if she knew he was there but did not recognize him.

"Elspeth," he said softly. She turned, as if hearing a distant echo. A smile came to her bloody lips that caused a cold knot to form in Slocum's belly. He ripped part of her nightgown off and wiped away the gore from her mouth.

"Elspeth!" He shook her now. Her head jerked back. The sharpness of the movement brought her around, but she was far from her usual alert self. The woman's mouth moved, and she lifted her trembling hands to her lips, rubbing over them.

"John, why are you here? My mother's outside. She . . ." Her words trailed off as she began taking in her surroundings. Elspeth turned and stared at him, eyes going wide. "What happened?"

"I don't know," Slocum said. He wanted to examine Barnsley's body again and see if the foreman's throat had been savaged by a wolf—or a human. From the amount of blood caking Elspeth's nightgown, Slocum thought she could have been responsible for Barnsley's ugly death. But how had a frail, sick young woman ever overpowered a trail-hardened cowhand like Quinton Barnsley? It seemed incredible.

Unless he had not expected a feral attack from someone he thought the world about. Someone he seemed overly protective about. Someone like Elspeth Kincannon.

"I have a terrible taste in my mouth, John. I don't understand what's going on." She seemed more animated for a moment, and then her senses faded into mist again.

"Elspeth, listen to me!" Slocum shook her, but this time it did not bring her around. He ripped more of her gown away and wiped off what blood he could. Slocum knew he might be doing something terrible, but in the past he had done worse than covering the trail of a possible murderer.

"I want to sleep," she said in her dreamy, distant voice.

Elspeth collapsed into Slocum's arms. He staggered, and then caught her up in his arms. He wanted to examine Barnsley's body, but getting Elspeth back to the house took priority. Stumbling through the dark, he found a small stream running near the house. He sucked in his breath, then pulled off the bloodstained nightgown from the woman's slender body. He had to peel dried strips of blood-soaked cloth away from her flesh. Every time he ripped free another section, Elspeth moaned. Eventually, he had her entirely naked.

Slocum remembered how it had been the last time he had seen her naked. It had been in Bannock and in bed. Nothing but delight had flowed from that meeting. Now he washed her from head to toe, getting every last drop of blood from her body. He left her nightgown in the stream as he worked, then turned to getting the spots out of it.

He held up the drenched nightgown and knew the spots would never come out. He had risked everything getting this far. Slocum decided to go for broke. Burying her nightgown deep enough that even a bloodhound would have trouble scenting it and digging it up, he gauged the distance between the stream and the ranch house.

"No way around it," he said. He awkwardly picked up the naked woman and started through the woods, hoping his sense of direction was good. It took the better part of an hour for him to carry Elspeth to the rear of the house. From inside he heard a loud argument, but could not make out the words. Taking this opportunity, he went to the window of Elspeth's bedroom and forced it open.

"In you go. You have to help me," he said, unable to hoist the woman through the window. She clumsily flailed about, but squirmed through the window amid loud banging and clattering.

Slocum put his hand to the ebony handle of his Colt when he heard something moving out in the yard. He relaxed when he saw that a horse had slipped its tether and moved about hunting for the water trough.

"John?" came the weak voice from inside the room. "Where am I?"

Slocum shinnied through the window and dropped in a crouch beside Elspeth. She lay on her side, curled up in a fetal position. Tears ran down her cheeks.

He laid his hand on her shoulder and said gently, "You're home, Elspeth. Get into bed. Where do you keep your nightgowns?" A young woman from such a rich family had to have more than one nightgown.

Slocum counted himself lucky that she crawled into bed on her own, even if she did not answer his question.

He hunted through drawers and a wardrobe without finding a fresh nightgown. Slocum gave up, deciding it had to be enough for him to pull the covers up over her shoulders.

"Thanks," Elspeth said dreamily. "Such a strange dream. Nice you're in it, John. I like you." With a tiny smile on her once-bloodstained lips, she slipped into a deep sleep. Slocum stood and watched her for several minutes until her slow, regular breathing assured him she was all right.

Or as good as she was likely to be.

Slocum pressed his ear against the door panel leading to the hall. The argument in the front room had died down. Slocum couldn't even tell who had been squabbling. Rather than risk being seen sneaking out the back way, Slocum retreated through Elspeth's bedroom window. He tried to pull the window down, but couldn't budge the sash. Leaving it, he decided that if questions were asked, it was more likely to be over Elspeth's lack of a nightgown.

There were some mysteries that simply didn't have answers. But Slocum vowed he would find out what had gone on with Barnsley.

He traced his steps back to where the man had been slaughtered like a cow. Any chance of examining Barnsley on his own had passed. Marshal Jenks and two deputies walked around the area. Jenks spotted Slocum as he came up.

"Found your horse, Slocum. Wondered if you'd gone off and gotten yourself killed like poor Quint."

"Did some tracking," Slocum said, hoping this would be the last of the questioning. It wasn't. For another twenty minutes the marshal interrogated him with pointed queries, until Slocum began to wonder if Jenks thought *he* had killed Barnsley.

"The sight of Quint really rattled Mr. Kincannon,"

Jenks finally said. "Glad he had the wit to send for me."

"He ride into town personally?"

Jenks shook his head. "Nope. Me and the deputies was ridin' out from town when the hand found us. The young 'un. What's his name?"

"Might have been the one they call Boots."

"That's the one, the kid with the fancy-ass boots. I swear, he thinks more of them than most folks do of their horse."

"Reckon I'd better get on back to the bunkhouse," Slocum said. "Done all I can out here."

"Sure you didn't see anything unusual, Slocum?"

"Not a thing," Slocum lied. Jenks stared at him skeptically, but said nothing more. Slocum left the lawmen, mounted, and rode back to the Sleepy K, wondering if Frank or Cora Kincannon had looked in on their daughter yet. And if they had, what would they think?

"I'm not sure it's a good idea for you to go hunting wolves anymore, Slocum. They're migrating to the south," Frank Kincannon said. No conviction rang in his words.

"That's not a pack of wolves doing the killing," Slocum said. "I think it's only one wolf, one that's developed a powerful taste for human blood."

His words caused Kincannon to stiffen and his face drain of blood.

"I'm pullin' back my bounty."

Slocum shrugged. "There's still a few dollars put up by other ranchers," he said.

"Isn't it about time for you to move on?" Kincannon asked. "You've done yeoman's work, but I'm sure the wolves are leaving. There won't be any more threat to us."

"In spite of what happened to your foreman?"

"Well, maybe," Kincannon said lamely.

"I'll be careful," Slocum said. "I won't shoot anything I don't identify first." This reassurance did nothing
to ease Kincannon's worry. The man started to say
something, probably intended to keep Slocum from his
hunt, but then subsided. Confusion washed over him.

Slocum swung into the saddle, made sure his Winchester rode easy in the sheath, then rode away from the
rancher. He was aware of other eyes on him, of Cora
Kincannon staring hotly at him from the porch, and William Kincannon sitting at the end of the front porch doing his best to look noncommittal. Where Frank was
upset, both of them seemed right pleased with themselves.

Slocum was having a hard time making sense out of
anything going on at the Sleepy K. He rode out, and
didn't kill his first wolf until three days later.

Slocum's belly growled. He was tired of living off the
sparse vegetation that turned brown with approaching
autumn and the occasional rabbit. Deer had vanished
from the countryside about the same time the wolves
moved in, Slocum guessed. A haunch of venison would
suit him well. Fact was, he even considered rustling one
of Kincannon's cows and diving into a thick slab of
good beefsteak.

He didn't. He hunted wolves, with diminishing luck.
The wolf pack that had tormented the countryside had
been killed off or moved on to better hunting—or both.
With a single skin draped over his saddlebags, Slocum
found himself riding into Bannock from the south. He
had made a huge circle around the Sleepy K, crossing
the full range once owned by Wellington, then made his
way south in an attempt to track the wolves.

His belly growling louder at the sight of a cafe, Slocum knew he would spend some of his hard-earned

money for a hot meal. He dismounted and went into the small diner. It was empty.

"Hello, anyone here?" he called. Dishes rattling in the back told him someone was there. He walked toward the rear, almost running into a middle-aged woman bustling from the kitchen, drying her hands as she came.

"Lordy, you scared me. Didn't expect anyone to come in."

"It's well nigh dinnertime," Slocum said.

"Clock time is not the same as dinnertime anymore. At least not here."

Slocum looked out into the street, realizing for the first time how deserted Bannock seemed.

"Where is everyone?" he asked.

"Set yourself down. If you want food, I can rustle up something. Won't be much, but it's likely to be better than a can of beans."

"Bannock looks like a ghost town," he repeated. "That what's cutting into your business?"

"People," she said, making it sound like a curse. "It's that crazy Cajun."

"Pierre?"

"That's the one. All the time he wanders around town, spewing out his poisonous talk about men who turn into wolves." She snorted in disgust. "Or women. Can you imagine?"

"He's saying a woman is a *loup-garou*?" Slocum sat up straighter. "Is he accusing anyone in particular?"

"All he wants is to sell his magic charms to ward off evil. *Gris-gris* he calls his stupid charms. He'd be better advised to go to church on Sunday and forget all that Devil-spawned stuff."

"Wouldn't make as much money that way," Slocum observed. The woman nodded curtly and vanished into the kitchen. Slocum heard rattling pans and low muttering as the woman worked, but the result proved excellent. Slocum had never tasted better pot roast, boiled potatoes, and fresh greens. When she insisted he have a second piece of peach pie, he was as content as he had been in weeks.

As he forked the last of the pie into his mouth, Slocum looked up and saw a deputy staring at him. At first he thought it was the one who had tried to run him out of town earlier. Then he decided this lawman only looked a little Like Deputy Hines.

"Slocum," the deputy said. "Marshal Jenks wants to talk to you. Now."

"Mighty fine," Slocum said to the woman. He paid and turned to the deputy. "I'm letting my dinner settle a spell."

"Let it settle on the way over to the courthouse. The marshal's got a powerful need to talk to you."

Slocum saw the man wasn't likely to be put off. He rose and settled his gunbelt around his middle. It was a mite tighter than when he had walked into the cafe. He headed for the courthouse at the end of town, aware of the deputy staying a few paces behind. Slocum's neck got an itchy feeling. He wondered if the deputy was walking with his hand on his six-shooter.

"Glad Lucas found you so fast," Marshal Jenks said. "We got a big problem, and you might be the gent who can help solve it."

"What can I do for you, Marshal?" Slocum perched on a chair near the door. The deputy faded into the shadows, but remained inside the courthouse. It was as deserted as the cafe had been.

"Hines rode out to the San Martino spread a day or two back to serve an eviction notice. Ain't seen hide nor hair of him since, and he ought to have been back by this morning at the latest."

"The ranch beyond the Wellington spread?" Slocum tried to picture the terrain. It looked as if the Sleepy K was the hub of a wheel of nothing but pure trouble. The wolves had decimated the herds and killed more than their share of men, but the ranch owners were turning tail and running.

"Hines was supposed to serve papers, evicting San Martino for not payin' on his taxes."

"So the ranch will go on the auction block?" Slocum struggled harder to picture the land being vacated. It all adjoined the Sleepy K. Anyone buying it up would have one hell of a fine ranch. Buying it for back taxes, or for the thousand that bought out Wellington, might make a man mighty rich in the blink of an eye.

Or the snap of a wolf's jaws.

"That's the way it works," Jenks said. He glanced toward his deputy, then back to Slocum. "You been out on the trail these past few days. You see Deputy Hines?"

"Reckon I'd know him if I saw him," Slocum allowed, "but I found it mighty lonely out there this time. Only bagged one wolf, and didn't see much else beside stragglers from the herds. It's getting to be time for the hands to round them up and get them ready for winter."

"You've seen Bannock. Half the town's upped and left. That damned Cajun rabble-rouser."

"I heard," Slocum said. "And I haven't seen your deputy out on the trail."

"If you do, tell him to get his worthless carcass back here. I'm not payin' him to lollygag."

Slocum agreed, rose, and left the deserted courthouse. Standing outside, he waited several minutes, and saw only a few stalwarts going into the saloons, ready for a night of drinking and gambling. Slocum walked slowly back to his horse, passing only a dozen men on the street. All seemed distant, suspicious. But he did hear Pierre bellowing out his litany of magic and death and how they could be turned away buying one of his special Cajun amulets.

Slocum mounted and rode slowly out of Bannock, wondering how long it would be until the entire town was deserted. The threat from the wolf packs had dwindled. The scarcity of the wolves on his last hunt proved that, but fear grew without bounds. A smart man could turn that fear to his own ends.

Having ridden the road many times, Slocum knew the shortcuts getting back to the Sleepy K, and took them all. It was just past three in the morning when he topped the rise overlooking the ranch house. A single lamp burned in Elspeth's window. Otherwise, no sign of life was evident around the house.

Slocum let his horse make its own way down the hillside. He stopped and walked the horse into the barn, making sure it was brushed down and fed before heading toward the bunkhouse. Slocum's steps slowed and he turned when he saw how Elspeth's window was wide open. He remembered the trouble he had had forcing the window when he had sneaked her back after Barnsley had been killed.

On silent feet, Slocum went to the window and peered into the bedroom. Elspeth lay on the bed, decked out in a new nightgown. She tossed restlessly, as if tormented by nightmare demons. Elspeth muttered, but Slocum could not make out the words.

Impulse overrode good sense. Slocum boosted himself into her bedroom and crossed the floor to sit on the edge of her bed.

He reached out and placed his hand on her forehead. A sliver of moonlight slanted in through the window, turning her flesh into something less than human. The clamminess Slocum found worried him. Elspeth had not improved from the night he had found her wandering insensate and drenched in blood.

Her eyelids flickered at his touch, and she opened eyes that appeared to burn with fever. It took a few seconds, but she finally recognized him.

"John, you're back. It's been weeks since I saw you."

"I can't stay. I just wanted to see how you were doing."

"Better, now that you're with me," she said. Elspeth wiggled about on the bed, curling up so she could rest her head on his leg. Her breathing turned more rhythmic and easier. Soon enough Elspeth slept more naturally than Slocum had seen her in some time.

"Good night," he said softly. He took her pillow, lifted her head, and then lowered her head onto it. She murmured again, but did not awaken. He stood and started for the window, almost falling flat on his face when he got his feet tangled in something on the bedroom floor.

Slocum crashed down to his knees. Elspeth turned restlessly in bed, but did not awaken. Cursing under his breath, Slocum tore at the garment tangling his boots. The moonlight coming in through the window caught something round and hard and metallic. Slocum lifted the vest after he got it off his feet, and stared at it.

The numerous bloodstains appeared jet black in the moonlight, but the deputy's badge remained bright silver. Slocum looked from the deputy's torn, bloodied vest and badge to the peacefully sleeping woman and wondered what the truth was.

10

Slocum stared at Frank Kincannon, not sure he had heard the man right.

"Well, Slocum? How about it? Forget hunting wolves. I want you to sign on as my new foreman."

"You want me to replace Barnsley?" This took Slocum by surprise. Of all the reasons he had thought Kincannon wanted to talk to him, this wasn't one. Barnsley had been devoted to the Kincannon family, and had seemed to look after the Sleepy K as if it had been his own. Slocum could never replace that kind of loyalty.

"Big boots to fill, I know," Kincannon said. "You're the man for it. I've seen how you work the herds. You're good. You have a way with the men too. You talk, they listen. And heaven knows, I need both talents right now."

"Is the herd still shrinking?" Slocum asked.

"I sent out two riders to get a count. One never returned. I think he kept on riding." Kincannon coughed and looked pained at having to admit any of his hands could be so disloyal. "At least, I hope that's what happened to Boots." The trapped expression on the rancher's face reminded Slocum that another man from

Bannock had been killed by wolves within the past week. "Trey came back with a count eighty short of what I expected."

"Mighty big loss, even if you think wolves are responsible," Slocum said. He had ridden four nights straight and had not seen a single wolf. Once he had heard distant howling, the shrill mocking laughter he had heard when he had started his hunt. Then it had shifted to a more natural wolf call. The moon had been rising, so Slocum had figured it was a lovelorn timber wolf hunting for a mate.

There hadn't been any kills he could confirm as being done by either a wolf or a wolf pack for a long time now.

"I'll make it worth your while, Slocum. You haven't been making a living wage hunting wolves for a while now. Fifty dollars a month, plus room, board, and gear."

"That's a mighty generous offer," Slocum said. It was more than the town marshal made. Fifty a month might be more than anyone in town earned, considering how Bannock had shrunk to being little more than a ghost town.

As this thought crossed his mind, Slocum snorted. One man in Bannock made more money. The crazy Cajun with his wild talk of *loup-garou* and magical charms made that much in a single night. Slocum glanced over Kincannon's shoulder to the front door of the ranch house. One of Pierre's intricately woven wreaths—*gris-gris*—hung there to ward off evil.

Slocum wasn't sure it was working.

"I'd offer more, but I'm not sure it's possible right now, the way things are and all," Kincannon said, looking more desperate than before. "I *need* your help. I do."

Slocum considered turning down the offer, then heard himself say, "I'll get a head count on the beeves as soon as I can. You have to know where you stand before winter.''

''Need to get in enough feed,'' Kincannon agreed. Then he brightened when he realized Slocum had taken on the job. He thrust out his hand. ''Thanks, Slocum. Thank you.''

Slocum shook hands, then turned from Kincannon, wondering at his own actions. Glancing over his shoulder as he want to the barn, Slocum saw Elspeth's bedroom window was again closed. Was she the reason he stayed? They had enjoyed one another's company back in Bannock, but since that single rainy night, the woman had been so distant, lost in a fever dream, if that was what it was.

Something more bothered Slocum about just leaving the Sleepy K. If he rode off, no one else would care about Elspeth's strange nightly peregrinations. Or the bloody nightgown she'd worn after Quinton Barnsley had died—or Deputy Hines's ripped, bloody vest. The deputy's body had never been found, but Slocum knew it was only a matter of time. If he could find anyone to bet with him, he'd put his money on Hines's body resembling that of the Sleepy K's former foreman.

A human mouth and sharp teeth would have ripped out the deputy's vulnerable throat. The best of trackers would find nothing but small human tracks around the body. And Elspeth would seem to be involved in that death too.

Slocum didn't have to see the body to know that that was what would happen.

''No,'' he said firmly. He couldn't believe the pale, trembling young woman had killed two powerful men.

''What's that, Slocum?'' called a cowhand.

''Get my horse saddled, Trey. I'm going out to check the herd.''

''Right away.'' The cowboy smiled crookedly.

"Reckon it's true then? You take the job as foreman?"

"Reckon it's true," Slocum said, wondering if everyone on the Sleepy K except him had known Kincannon was going to make the offer. He rode out, aware of eyes watching him. He would have felt better if it had been a vulture waiting for him to die rather than Cora Kincannon staring silently at him from the house.

He wheeled his horse in a tight circle, studying the ground where it had been chopped up by cattle's hooves. From the look of the grass, at least twenty head had moved along here at a good clip. Estimating the length of the stride on the beeves, Slocum wondered if they had been stampeding.

Or were being herded.

He couldn't be sure, but thought he saw shod hoofprints mingled with those of the cattle. Following the trail left by the cattle, Slocum soon found himself riding in the direction of the San Martino spread. He broke off the hunt for the cattle, trotted to the top of a low rise, and got a better grip on where he was. Still on the Sleepy K, he figured. He guessed that the Wellington spread lay directly east and the San Martino to the west, a thin island of Kincannon's ranch separating the two.

Slocum picked up the trail again and began looking for the cattle themselves after another mile. The spoor left was fresh, cow chips left within the hour from the way the flies swarmed. He didn't see the cattle, and became warier when obvious shod hoofprints rode in from the north to join the herd—rustlers moving the herd along.

The countryside had turned hillier, but offered better grazing than on the Sleepy K. Slocum considered finding another rise and seeing what he could uncover, but changed his mind when he heard the loud whinnying of horses ahead.

He dropped from horseback and took cover a ways from the trail. Soothing his horse, Slocum turned his attention to the riders coming from higher ground. Three men rode shoulder to shoulder, arguing among themselves.

"More!" complained the man in the center of the trio. "He wants more cattle. He think stealing that many's easy?"

"What do you care?" snapped the rider on the right. "We're gettin' paid good for this."

"And the law's practically gone to ground." The third rider laughed harshly. "When's the last time a deputy came ridin' out alone? They're afraid of the *loup-garou*!"

All three laughed at that, strengthening Slocum's suspicion that the Cajun was part of a scheme to steal men's ranches and cattle.

The middle rider held up his hand and stopped the other two. He tipped his head to the side, listening intently. With a hand motion, he sent one rider to the left of the trail and the other to the right. Reaching down, he pulled out his rifle and cocked it.

Slocum faded into shadows, wondering how he had given himself away. Then he knew. His tracks along the road. The rustlers had done their best to conceal their hoofprints among those of the cattle. Grabbing his own rifle caused his horse to rear and kick out.

The sound wouldn't have been noticed if the three rustlers hadn't been alerted. Bullets ripped through the foliage of the bushes around him. Slocum let his horse run, hoping this would distract the rustlers and give him a chance to ambush them.

The three worked together well, covering each other as they advanced through the undergrowth. No needless chatter passed between them now as they fixed their full attention on finding and killing him. Slocum started to cock his Winchester, then stopped. The sound would alert them. He lay the rifle on the ground and drew his Colt Navy. It was single-action, but he could get off several shots faster with it than he could with his rifle if he stayed flat on his belly.

The leader came into view. Slocum never hesitated because it was only a matter of seconds before the man rode on top of him. Slocum's quickly aimed bullet took off the rustler's hat, sending it spinning into the air.

The man responded instantly, getting off three shots that forced Slocum to roll and take shelter behind a thick-boled oak. He swung up his rifle and levered in a round. The sound of the working mechanism echoed through the woods like thunder. Both Slocum's target and another of the rustlers homed in on him. Their rifles spitting foot-long tongues of flame, they forced him to retreat, to find cover behind another tree.

His back pressed against the rough trunk of a tree, Slocum caught his breath. The men were closing in on him, flanking him, and sure to kill him unless he acted fast.

He fired to the left of the tree, then to the right, keeping the men at bay. Then he clambered up the tree like a squirrel and flopped belly down along a high limb. Slocum wondered how he kept the leaves from shaking. His hands trembled, and sweat dripped into his eyes. He sucked in a calming breath and bided his time. The rustlers did not come into his line of fire, though.

Slocum wondered if they were waiting for him to get antsy and show himself like some greenhorn, or if they had retreated. He listened hard, but heard nothing but the sounds of wind through the leaves and occasional animals moving again. Wiggling along the limb brought him to the tree trunk. Slocum risked dropping, rifle clutched in his hands and ready to shoot his way out of a tight spot.

The rustlers were nowhere to be seen.

Slocum shook his head in amazement. Nothing made sense. Rustlers who vanished, herds that vanished, wolves that vanished—and still the killing and stealing went on. Cautiously, Slocum explored the immediate arca, and found no trace of the three rustlers. He heaved a deep breath and went hunting for his runaway horse, finally catching it almost a mile deeper into the woods.

"What now?" Slocum wondered. If he found the tracks leading up the narrow pass and down into what was probably another meadow on the far side of the ridge, he would walk into a ring of rustlers' guns. He sighed. He was foreman of the Sleepy K. His duty was obvious.

"Marshal Jenks," he decided. "I fetch the lawman and we come out here and . . . find nothing." Slocum felt dejected. The rustlers were unlikely to stick around. He hadn't thought they were yellow-bellied cowards, but they must have been. Three against one was odds even the worst of gutless backshooters would take. Unless something had spooked them.

Slocum returned to the spot where he had first come across the rustlers, and stared up into the saddleback where they must have retreated. Looking around slowly, he saw nothing to run them off.

"Maybe they thought I was part of a posse," Slocum said to himself. Whatever it had been, he knew it had saved his hide. Pulling on the reins, he headed back toward the Sleepy K. Getting Jenks to ride out and investigate didn't seem to be reasonable, not if the rustlers hightailed it for the high country, but he could get several of the Sleepy K hands and come back. After all, it was Frank Kincannon's cattle being stolen, and he was foreman now.

Slocum slowed, and eventually reined back before he had ridden two miles. The *clop-clop* of an approaching horse alerted him to the presence of another rider long before he saw who sat astride the big chestnut gelding.

"John!" Elspeth cried, waving to him. She snapped the reins and got her gelding trotting toward him. Slocum swung from side to side to be sure the rustlers weren't anywhere to be seen. He didn't want Elspeth caught in a cross fire. But the rustlers were long gone.

"What are you doing out here?" he asked.

"I got to feeling better," Elspeth said. "Restless and cooped up. I don't know how long I was sick, but it got to the point where I had to get some fresh air."

"Glad to see you out and about," Slocum said. "I want to get back to the house. Why don't we ride back together?"

"Do we have to go straight back?" she asked, the impish look in her eyes that Slocum remembered so well from their passionate night in Bannock. While she was still pale, color had returned to her cheeks, and she seemed more animated.

"Reckon not," Slocum said, coming to a quick decision. He had questions he wanted answered. He was more likely to get them from Elspeth if they were away from her parents.

"You seem upset, John. What's happened?"

He ignored the question and asked one of his own. "What do you remember of being sick?"

"Why, there were nightmares. Awful ones. But mostly, I don't remember anything." Elspeth laughed and said, "I am so happy to be feeling better. I seemed to have horrible tastes in my mouth much of the time. That I remember."

He stared at her and wondered if she remembered anything about Quinton Barnsley or Deputy Hines. He asked.

"I heard about poor Quint," she said. "Uncle Will

told me wolves had killed him. But I know nothing about the deputy. Why do you ask?''

''Nothing,'' he said.

''Let's take a break. I've been in the saddle too long, and I'm not used to it.'' She lifted up slightly and rubbed her curvy rump. Elspeth was obviously aware of Slocum's reaction, because she repeated the action, then sank down.

He dismounted, and then held the reins to Elspeth's horse as she put her hands on his shoulders to jump down. She brushed against him as she dropped, her lush breasts pressing warmly along his arm. Elspeth did not shy away. If anything, she moved closer. Even through the thick layers of clothing, Slocum felt the hard points of the woman's nipples squeezing into his chest.

''I've missed you, John. I wish I hadn't been so ill.'' Her bright eyes shone with intelligence and need. Gone was the flat, almost dead appearance of earlier weeks.

''You've made a speedy recovery,'' Slocum said.

''For the life of me, I don't know why since Mama ran out of medicine. I suppose it was just time for me to feel better.''

Slocum sucked in his breath.

''That's not all you're feeling,'' he said. Her fingers moved across the buckle holding his gunbelt, then worked lower. She began massaging the lump she found growing at his crotch.

''What am I feeling?'' she asked coyly.

''I think you're feeling your oats,'' Slocum said. He kissed her. Their lips crushed together, and he forgot all about how this mouth had been drenched with Barnsley's blood. All he tasted was the sweet wine of mutual desire.

Elspeth's lips parted slightly, and her pink tongue darted out to tease Slocum's. Their tongues played hide-and-seek a few minutes as their hands roved over each other's willing bodies. Somehow, Slocum found himself free of his shirt and Elspeth working on the buttons holding up his jeans.

"Not fair," he said. "I haven't even started on your clothes yet."

"Do it," she said, her breasts rising and falling with desire. She closed her eyes, tossed her head back, and let the gentle breeze catch her long dark hair like some banner of surrender. Slocum reached out and began unfastening the ties and buttons on Elspeth's dress, until he reached the next layer of frilly undergarment.

"Let me, John," she said. "It takes forever to get it on. I don't want to take forever getting it off!"

Slocum watched in growing fascination as Elspeth stripped off her garments and finally stood naked to the waist. She swayed slightly from side to side, causing her breasts to jiggle. Soft sunlight touched her naked breasts, turning them into something delightful and deliciouslooking. Slocum reached out and cupped her twin glories. She sighed and moved closer.

He kissed each of the breasts, and then worked his hands around behind her, lifting her skirts until he found bare warm flesh.

She stepped forward and forced him backward. Slocum sank down, and ended up on his back. Elspeth knelt down, lifting her skirts out of the way as she tugged at the thick, hard shaft of manhood jutting up from Slocum's groin.

Elspeth settled down. He felt the tip of his shaft touch the lust-dampened nether lips. Then the aroused woman sank down, taking him fully into her most intimate recess.

Slocum groaned and began bucking, moving in and out of her although she weighed him down. He reached up and wrapped his arms around her. The upward motion carried Elspeth backward and onto her back. Her legs parted amid a rustling of her skirts. Slocum repositioned himself a little, and then began moving with more strength, more determination, as his desire for her mounted.

"Oh, John, I've missed you so. I wish I hadn't been sick for so long. I need this. It makes me come alive! *You* make me feel completely alive!" She let out a low moan of joy as he began moving faster and faster. She responded fully, lifted her knees up on either side of his body, and began striving with him until they both arrived at the pinnacle of human pleasure at the same instant.

Slocum sank down and pulled Elspeth close to him. She fit nicely into the circle of his arms. They lay together, enjoying the afterglow of their lovemaking, neither saying a word.

Slocum wanted to ask about so much, but did not. He didn't want to ruin the moment. There might not be many more of them. Whatever was going on at the Sleepy K was running out of control now.

11

"You got better when you stopped taking the medicine your ma gave you?" Slocum frowned as he considered this curious occurrence while they rode back toward the ranch. Medicine wasn't supposed to make a patient sicker; it was supposed to heal. "Maybe you and the medicine didn't agree." Maybe this was the cause of the argument between Barnsley and Cora Kincannon. The foreman might have known the medicine was harming Elspeth instead of helping her.

"I don't remember much of it, John," Elspeth said cheerfully. "I don't want to. I want to enjoy this fine day. I miss being out in the sun and air." She turned and almost shyly added, "And I miss being with you."

Slocum said, "You recall me coming to your bedroom a few nights back?"

"I had a dream with you in it. A real dream, not one of my nightmares. But I know I'd recollect it if you came to bed with me. How could a girl forget such a thing?" She batted her eyelashes at him coquettishly.

"Didn't say I went to bed with you, just that I was in your room. You were still under the weather, I guess." He saw she had no memory of him or Barnsley, or even of the bloody vest with the tin deputy's badge pinned on it. She wanted only to rejoice now in being out of the stuffy bedroom and under the bright, early fall Montana sun.

All Slocum wanted to do was figure out if she was a crazed killer. Looking at her now, he could not believe it, even if the evidence pointed in that direction. Without knowing he did so, he reached up and touched the silver bullet Kincannon had given him the first night he had gone wolf hunting. A silver bullet. According to legend, the only way a werewolf could be killed.

A *loup-garou*.

"Why are you out here—not that I mind," Elspeth said quickly. "I count it as my lucky day our paths crossed as they did."

"You don't know I'm the new foreman?"

"What! Oh, wonderful." Elspeth settled down and pursed her lips in thought. "What happened to Quint? Did his injured arm get to acting up on him? He's been the Sleepy K foreman since I was eleven or twelve. Or are you just acting foreman until he heals up?"

"He's dead, Elspeth. A wolf got him. Deputy Hines is dead too. And a lot of other good men. Every last one of them looks to be the victim of a man-killer wolf." He watched her reaction carefully. If she was faking it, she was a better actress than any he had ever seen in a stage play.

"No, John, it can't be true. Why, Quint was like one of the family. He can't be dead."

"Your mother sent him on her errands a lot, did she?"

The question took Elspeth by surprise. "Why, no, I don't remember any in particular. He worked for us all. I suppose he might have run a special errand for Mama now and again, but he was usually too busy with real work. He would have sent one of the hands, maybe."

Elspeth frowned and chewed on her lower lip, finally coming to the conclusion that Slocum was interrogating her and that she wasn't too happy about it. "What a strange question. Why did you ask?"

"Nothing," Slocum said, remembering he hadn't called on the pharmacist in Bannock to find what Barnsley had brought back to Cora Kincannon. He was getting the idea that Barnsley wasn't as much a family friend as Elspeth thought—or as much of a friend for *her*, at least.

"Good," she said. "This is too perfect a day to ruin asking silly questions." She settled down and rode in silence for a mile or more before saying in a low voice, "Quint's really dead?"

"He is," Slocum said. "I'm sorry."

Elspeth said nothing more until they rode up to the house. She smiled weakly at him, looking tired from the ride.

"I'm more tuckered out than I thought. Perhaps I'm not as well as I felt earlier."

"Maybe the bad news didn't set well with you," Slocum said. "I didn't mean to spring it on you. I thought you knew."

"No one told me. Poor Quint. He was a good man."

Before Slocum could say a word, William Kincannon and his sister-in-law burst from the house like a pair of chickens chased by a hound dog. They were so intent on getting out, Slocum thought the door might sail off its hinges as it slammed back.

"Elspeth! There you are! You had me worried. Are you all right?" William Kincannon looked from the pale woman to Slocum, as if accusing him of kidnapping her. Slocum wondered if that might not be a good idea, considering his growing suspicions.

"I'm fine, Uncle Will. Mr. Slocum's been kind to ride back with me. I'm tired." She tied the reins in a half hitch, then stared at her uncle. "Why didn't you tell me Quint was dead?"

"You—" Cora Kincannon barely held her anger in check as she stepped toward Slocum. Her fists clenched, and she would have hit him if she had been closer.

"You have no right to meddle in our business," Will Kincannon said to Slocum. Slocum didn't miss how Kincannon had to look at Cora before he spoke.

"Uncle Will, please! It's not John's fault. He thought I knew already. Why didn't you tell me?"

"You're too weak, my dear," Kincannon said. "Go on into the house with your mother. You need to rest."

"Very well. I could use some rest. And food. I am actually hungry for the first time in—well, I can't remember!"

"I'll get you something, my dear. And I got some more medicine from town. It's my fault I didn't give you your dose this morning, and you took off like you did. I'll give you two spoonfuls to take with your food, just to be on the safe side."

Slocum started to call out to Elspeth to avoid the medicine, but William Kincannon stepped up and thrust out his chin in an aggressive fashion, as if daring Slocum to make something of it.

"What is Miss Elspeth suffering from that you need to give her medicine all the time?" Slocum asked.

The question confused Kincannon for a moment. Then he grew even more belligerent and shoved Slocum back. Kincannon's eyes widened a little when he saw Slocum was not a man to push around. Slocum didn't tense, he didn't go for the Colt Navy in its cross-draw holster, but he did change the set of his body enough to show Kincannon how close to death he'd just come for his impetuous action.

"You let her family worry about Elspeth's condition. It's none of your business." William Kincannon's order rang hollow in the face of Slocum's quiet defiance.

"Where's Mr. Kincannon? I don't see him around."

"He's out riding the fence, looking for strays, whatever needs doing." Kincannon cleared his throat and summoned up his courage to beard Slocum again. "You're only a hired hand, Slocum. You don't go asking a passel of questions."

"Mr. Kincannon made me foreman. That gives me the right to ask more questions than some cowpuncher."

"Not as long as I'm around," Kincannon said, getting his dander up. "My brother allows too much impertinence from his employees."

"Then it's a good thing you don't have any say in running the Sleepy K," Slocum said coldly. Before Kincannon could do more than sputter at this insolence, Slocum walked away and led his horse toward the barn. He seethed with anger, but cooled down as he tended the horse. When he finished giving the trusty animal a bucket of oats, he went to the barn door and stared at the house.

It had seemed so peaceful when he had first seen it. Now he knew that the insides were festering, and the people there little better than maggots. Slocum wondered how he could get Elspeth out again. When Cora and William came onto the porch and argued, keeping their voices low but obviously not agreeing, he knew there was no chance in Hell he could pry the lovely woman free.

If Cora had given her daughter more of her "medicine," Elspeth might again be locked away in a drugged stupor.

"What's so interesting?" asked Trey. The young cowboy sauntered up, thumbs tucked into his belt, hip cocked to one side.

"Them," Slocum said, jerking his thumb in the direction of the Kincannons.

"Quite a pair, they are," Trey said, grinning crookedly. He spat, then wiped his lips. "I've always wondered if Mr. Kincannon knows what goes on between them."

Slocum wasn't surprised that others on the Sleepy K knew William Kincannon and Cora acted like they were more than in-laws.

"You have a six-shooter?" Slocum asked.

"Somewhere. Might be rusty since I don't carry it much."

"Get it. And if you have a rifle and ammo, bring those along too. We're going to hunt us up some rustlers," Slocum said. There was nothing more he could do here. Retrieving eighty or more head of cattle for Frank Kincannon would go a long way toward remedying the sorry situation on the Sleepy K.

"Why not go fetch the marshal?"

"I'm not sure what we're going to find, other than trouble," Slocum said. "They might have lit out, and there won't be anything to find. Or I might be wrong about these particular gents being rustlers."

"But you don't think so?" asked Trey.

Slocum remembered the bullets flying around his head as he dove for cover in the undergrowth just below the saddleback.

"Not a chance," he said.

"Never been on this range," Trey said anxiously. The young cowboy had grown increasingly anxious when they'd left the Sleepy K and entered the San Martino spread. "Don't see why rustlers would bring our beeves this way."

"I don't either, but there must be a reason," Slocum said. He was tired of finding more questions without solving earlier problems. Something told him a bucket of answers would be dumped on him if he located the rustlers and the cattle they had been purloining from the Sleepy K.

"I'm not much for putting up fences, but we're trespassing," Trey said. "I know San Martino, and he's a decent fella."

"Spread doesn't belong to him anymore," Slocum said. "It was sold. Like the Wellington ranch."

"The new owner might not like us poking around his territory," Trey said. Slocum stared at him, wondering what was wrong. He seldom saw any cowboy worried over trespassing. That was the way sodbusters talked.

"Up there might be eighty head or more of Kincannon cattle," Slocum said, pointing up the draw to the saddleback. "I don't know the land, but from the look of the hills, I'd say a big meadow stretches on the far side."

"Just the sort of place to graze stolen cattle till you can run their brand and move 'em to a railhead," Trey said.

"You know more about rustling than you care to admit," Slocum said. Trey stiffened, and his hand went to the six-gun thrust into his belt. "It doesn't bother *me*," Slocum added. After he said this, Trey relaxed a mite. Slocum wondered if a wanted poster might not hang in some marshal's office with the young cowboy's picture on it. When Slocum had asked him to come along, Trey might have thought he was being accused of rustling his boss's cattle.

"You seem to know a bit about the process too," Trey said.

"Never was any good at running a brand, but I know how to move a herd a hundred miles in two days. Even a posse on fresh horses has a time keeping up." Slocum pulled his horse to a halt so he could look down into the gentle bowl of a valley beyond the saddleback. "Been a spell since I rode the outlaw trail, though."

"Me too," Trey said. "Since I came to work at the Sleepy K, I been treated decent-like. I don't want to do anything to jeopardize that."

"You'll be a hero if we find the cattle stolen from the Sleepy K," Slocum said. Even ten or twenty head added up to a significant recovery, making it well worth their while.

"There's the trail, Slocum," Trey said, pointing. Slocum had already seen it. The winding road over the hills had been rocky, and the cattle hooves had vanished in the gravelly stretches, but once they reached the richer earth of the valley, the hoofprints reappeared. "Looks to be a lot of beeves."

Slocum paid less attention to the trail and more to where they rode. They were exposed. It would take quite a marksman to shoot them at long range, but Slocum didn't want to ride into a trap—or find his retreat cut off because some sentry spotted them.

They could see anyone a mile off. The same worked for the rustlers. He and Trey had nowhere to hide as they rode through the valley.

"You know something, Slocum?" asked Trey. "I think there might be a rail spur at the other end of the valley. I was talking with the stationmaster in Bannock a while back, and he said something once about a spur running down into the San Martino spread."

"Convenient place to load on stolen cattle," Slocum observed. He could see rustled beeves from all over the area being herded down this valley, and grazed to fatten them, and then, with their brands changed, shipped out to a legitimate buyer. The problem with most stolen cattle was getting rid of them. Most ranchers refused to buy cattle without clear origins, and selling to slaughterhouses could be risky. Slocum had seen an army of Pinkertons perched on fences outside stockyards looking like so many crows as they hunted for rustled stock.

Whoever was behind this rustling could sell at reasonable prices and make a considerable profit at it. More than this, the leader of the outlaws had enough money to buy up two ranches, and might be trying to buy the Sleepy K.

"Wolves," Slocum muttered. *"Loup-garou."* He shook his head in disgust. It hardly mattered if the rustlers only took advantage of the wolf pack that had ravaged the countryside, or if they had brought in Pierre and thought it up all by themselves.

Men had still died, and Slocum doubted the wolves were responsible for very many of those deaths, if any.

"Don't see our cows, Slocum. Should we keep going or do you want to head back and get the marshal?"

"I want proof. Jenks is hardheaded. He'd want to be certain he wasn't wasting his time riding out from town. After all, there's no sheriff to enforce the law out here."

"There's enough tracks around here to convince any lawman," Trey insisted. "Do we need to find the cattle too?"

"Probably," Slocum said, more alert now. He saw nothing unusual, and heard nothing in the grave-silent valley. Maybe it was this emptiness that spooked him, or perhaps the sixth sense that had kept him alive through the war now spoke its quiet warning to him.

"We're not far from the end of the valley," Trey said: "We ought to see the spur line any time now." His voice took on an edge. The young man was turning edgier too. His hand moved in the direction of the pistol butt, although he did not draw.

"Something eating at you?" Slocum asked.

"It's too quiet," Trey said. "I don't like this. I don't see anyone, but there's someone watching us."

Slocum nodded. The cowboy had good instincts. He hoped the young man also had courage. Bullets were going to fly before they got out of the valley.

"There's the railroad spur," Slocum said, the twin steel tracks gleaming brightly in the sun. No rust on those rails. He rode up and let his horse dance over the tracks and between the ties.

"Slocum, take a look at this," Trey called from a ways down the line. Slocum trotted over and stared.

"A lot of cows were loaded," Slocum decided. "Maybe the eighty or so Mr. Kincannon thinks are missing from the Sleepy K."

"Might be even more. Look how far back the trampled area goes," Trey said, starting to explore. Slocum started to yell a warning, then reacted with his six-shooter instead.

He drew and fired three times as fast as he could cock the hammer and pull the trigger. The .36-caliber slugs sailed past Trey. The cowboy fought to keep his horse from rearing. This bucking saved his life. Twin tongues of muzzle flash stabbed out from behind a tumble of rocks fifty yards away.

"Get down," Slocum yelled. "They're behind those rocks. This way!" Slocum shoved his Colt Navy back into his holster. The range was too great for a handgun. He pulled out his rifle, settled down, and squeezed off a round. The slug whined off the rock, and a loud yelp of pain was his reward for good shooting.

"You winged one of the bastards!" cried Trey. He put his heels to his horse's heaving flanks and galloped toward a pile of firewood, possibly cut for refueling the engine coming down this spur to pick up the rustled cattle.

Slocum joined Trey behind the waist-high stack of cut wood. Splinters began flying all around them as the ambushers got down to serious shooting.

"We flushed someone out," Trey said. "Are they rustlers?"

"They're someone who wants us dead," Slocum said.

"Doesn't much matter beyond that." He poked his head out for a quick look, and took a bullet through the brim of his Stetson. He ducked back and sat with his back to the wood.

"What are we going to do?" Trey asked. "I have a rifle, but not that much ammo. How about you?"

"Not enough for a full-fledged fight. We don't even know how many of them are out there."

"We can run for it. We'll have a clear run all the way back to the Sleepy K," said Trey.

"I don't like running from a fight," Slocum said, but the cowboy had a good point. This wasn't the time or place to have a showdown.

"I don't like being buzzard bait," Trey said hotly. "You say the word, we fight. Otherwise, let's get the hell out of here!"

Slocum considered their position and the seemingly endless supply of ammunition being blasted in their direction by the ambushers. He waited a few seconds, then said, "There are only two of them. No other way to interpret their fire."

"So we rush them?"

"Why not?" Slocum said. He took a deep breath and pointed to the right, showing Trey where to go to flank their attackers. Then he levered in a round, hefted his rifle, and let out a loud shout.

Slocum bolted from behind the woodpile, firing as he ran. He heard Trey shouting and firing his six-shooter as he headed in the other direction. They'd either flush the two backshooters or they'd die trying.

Slocum wasn't sure which it would be when he saw how far he had to run before reaching cover. Bullets started kicking up dirt all around his feet and buzzing past his ears, and he began doubting how smart this offensive was.

He dug in his toes and ran even faster. It was all he could do to stay alive.

12

A bullet struck Slocum's boot heel and sent him tumbling head over heels. He hit the ground hard, and tried to keep his momentum going so he wouldn't flop about helplessly in the line of fire. He almost made it. He kicked and squirmed and dodged more bullets that ripped through his shirt and pants leg, some hotly touching skin, before he got behind a fallen log. Seeing how rotted the log was, Slocum kept moving—and that saved his life.

Slugs ripped through the log and cut into the space where Slocum had rested for a few brief seconds. He kept wiggling on his belly until he came to a sturdier log. Only then did he drop his rifle on top of the downed tree trunk and take careful aim. His finger came back slowly, and he got off another shot that wounded one bushwhacker.

Slocum swung the rifle around to cover Trey, but the young cowhand had already gone to earth, finding shelter behind a medium-sized rock. He waved to Slocum, who signaled he was all right too.

For several minutes, neither Slocum and Trey nor the two bushwhackers ventured out. Then Slocum figured it was time to act. He got his feet under him, wobbling slightly where the boot heel had been blown off, and sprinted straight for the rocks shielding the ambushers. He ran with his rifle level and ready to fire at any sign of movement.

He crashed into the side of the rock, glanced over his shoulder to be sure Trey was in position to cover him, then swarmed up and over.

Slocum had worried that the bushwhackers had retreated to safer positions. They had. Both opened up on him simultaneously, driving him back to the safety of the far side of the rock. But by concentrating their fire on his abortive attempt to take them, they ignored Trey.

The cowboy pounded hard around the far side of the rock and got a clean shot at one would-be killer. Trey's six-shooter blared, and the air filled with white smoke from the muzzle. But he tried to fire a second time, and his hammer fell on a spent cartridge.

"Slocum!" he shouted before the bullet took him in the leg. Trey fell heavily and pulled himself out of the line of fire.

Slocum tried again to make a frontal assault, and again was driven back by heavy fire. He rebounded, spun around the rock, and dropped beside Trey. The cowboy worked to tear the heavy denim of his jeans to see what damage had been done to his leg.

"Better tie a tourniquet around it," Slocum said, taking part of the man's pants leg and ripping it into a long strip.

"They'll get away." Trey grimaced as Slocum applied pressure to the tourniquet.

"Then they'll get away. I wounded one of them. You got one too, didn't you?"

"Probably. I saw him grab his side. That makes them easier to get if you go now. I'll be fine. Not going to

bleed to death with such a tight tourniquet on.'' Trey
made a wry face.

"Reload," Slocum ordered. He waited until the
young man's six-gun was ready for action again before
he left him. Too many times he had tried a full-out assault and had been driven back. It was time now for
stealth.

On his belly, crawling like an Apache, Slocum made
his way through the dirt and dust, leaving behind a trail
of bloody mud from his own scratches. He skirted the
area where he thought the ambushers had holed up, circling until he came up on the far side of a good-sized
hill. Slocum got to his feet and went to the top of the
rise, falling forward, rifle leveled and ready to fire.

He sighted in on . . . emptiness.

"Damnation," he grumbled. Working his way down
the hill to avoid being a target in case he had missed the
pair of bushwhackers, he examined the area where the
men had fired. He found empty brass casings from their
rifles, and even a few drops of blood on the rocks and
in the grass. But of the men, there was no trace.

Slocum sat with his back against the rock and looked
around. He had circled, so they hadn't gotten past him.
Trey hadn't fired, so they had not tried to duplicate Slocum's suicidal straight-ahead attack and overpower the
cowboy. That left only one way—to the left.

"Slocum, what's going on?" Trey shouted.

"Lost them," Slocum said, hating to admit it. He hobbled along, studying the ground. The boot prints he
found were wide-spaced, showing the two men had run
hard and fast to get away while he was wasting his time
circling around them. They had been cunning and hadn't
tried retreating toward him. If they had, he would have
bagged the pair of them as they came up the slope into
his sights.

He made his way more slowly, then stopped when he

heard the thunder of hooves in the distance. The two had gotten clean away. Cursing a blue streak, he returned to where Trey was trying to stand, supporting himself against a rock.

"Sit down and rest," Slocum advised.

"You lost them?"

"They're gone," Slocum said. "Fact is, we're lucky *we* got away. If they'd been better shots, we'd both be pushing up daisies by now." He worked on the heel of his boot, trying to fix a piece of wood he'd cut from a fallen tree limb to fit over the nails sticking out. It didn't work well, but it worked well enough so he wouldn't limp as he walked. The new heel might actually hold his foot in the stirrup when he got back into the saddle too.

"What are we going to do, Slocum? Because they shot at us doesn't prove anything more 'n we'd found out already."

"Does to me," Slocum said, testing his whittling handiwork. He walked back and forth a few paces. The heel wouldn't last long, but might get him back to town, where he could get a cobbler to work on it. "I might have been wrong before about this being where the rustled cattle were put on a freight car, but odds are against it now."

"Seems you're right, but you were right saying Marshal Jenks would want hard evidence. We don't have it, unless you count the hole in my leg leakin' blood." Trey studied Slocum for a few seconds and added, "You have your share of scratches too."

Together they hobbled to get their horses.

"Feel like the lame leading the lame," Trey joked. He swung into the saddle, made a face as pain hit him, then settled down. It took Slocum a bit longer to catch his horse and mount.

"We might be ambushed on the way out of here, so

keep an eye peeled,'' Slocum warned. They rode down the middle of the valley, retracing the path they had followed to get to the railroad spur—and the ambush. Slocum saw nothing moving anywhere in the valley, much less a gunman intent on ventilating him.

They reached the saddleback and had started down the far side, heading for Sleepy K land, when Trey straightened and pointed ahead. Slocum nodded. He had already seen the dust of a solitary rider working his way along a line of fence meant to separate the San Martino property from the Sleepy K, and guessed it might be Frank Kincannon.

''That's the boss,'' Trey said, finally recognizing the rider.

''No need to hurry since *he's* not,'' Slocum said. He was feeling achy and tired, but he worried more about Trey passing out on him. The cowboy's leg continued to dribble blood in spite of the tourniquet. He needed the doctor in Bannock to tend it.

They hailed Frank Kincannon when they got within a hundred yards. The man turned in the saddle, and Slocum wondered at the set to his body. Kincannon slumped like a man already defeated. Something more than downed fence worried him.

''Rustlers, Mr. Kincannon,'' bubbled Trey. ''Back there. Up on the San Martino ranch. That old railroad spur. You know the one I mean? They—''

''Whoa, son. Not so fast. Why don't you tell me what's going on, Slocum?''

Slocum's distant appraisal proved even more accurate as he neared Kincannon. The man's face was pinched and drawn, as if he was in emotional pain. He seemed to have difficulty in keeping his attention on the matter at hand, as serious as it was. Kincannon kept turning and looking back in the direction of the ranch house, as if he could see it through several miles of woods and hills.

A crazy thought flashed through Slocum's head that Kincannon might have been one of those trying to dry-gulch him and Trey. Then he discarded the notion. Kincannon showed no sign of a bloody fight. Slocum was sure he had winged both gunmen. For all Kincannon's distress, he wasn't injured and his clothing was fresh and clean, as if he had just ridden out from the ranch.

"We ought to fetch the marshal and let him look over the spur," Slocum said. "He won't find the rustlers, but maybe he can telegraph on down the line and find where our beeves went."

"You certain our cattle were moved out from there?"

"Well, no," Slocum admitted, "but it's worth getting the marshal anyway. Trey is pretty badly shot up."

"Not much of a crime can be proved unless you got a good look at the men doing the shooting. Either of you get a clear view of them?"

Trey and Slocum both shook their heads.

"Then there's no call to involve the marshal. We have enough men left on the Sleepy K to round up our own beeves, should we find them. And we can plug this valley up tight so no more of my cattle are stolen."

"No marshal?" Trey asked, startled. "We can stop them, Mr. Kincannon, if we—"

"No lawmen," Kincannon said angrily.

"You want me to keep poking around to see what evidence I can get against them?" asked Slocum.

"Yes, you and Trey and any of the other men you want to recruit. But keep the marshal out of this. Don't mention it around town either."

"All right," Slocum said.

"I have to get back to the house. It'll be dark soon. You get Trey on into Doc Talbot and let the old sawbones fix him up. I need all the hands I can get in good condition.''

Slocum shrugged and turned toward a game trail that would take them to the main road into Bannock. Before he had ridden ten feet, Kincannon called, ''And the wolves, Slocum, the wolves. Don't forget them. Watch out for the wolves.''

Slocum stared at Frank Kincannon and wondered what was going on. Tears ran down the man's leathery cheeks. Then the rancher trotted off, heading back in the direction of the ranch.

''He'll live. Hell, I don't even have to whack off his damn leg,'' Dr. Talbot said, wiping his hands on a carbolic-soaked rag. He tossed the rag into a bucket, sniffed like a dog a few times, and then returned to his desk and the newspaper he had been reading.

''Can he ride on back to the Sleepy K?'' asked Slocum.

''Ride? After what you did to him?'' Talbot snorted in disgust. ''He'd better spend the night. Let him ride out in the morning—in a wagon, not on horseback. He's going to need a week or two convalescing. That a problem, Slocum?'' Talbot leaned forward belligerently, daring Slocum to contradict him.

''No,'' was all Slocum said.

''Then get the hell out of here and let me work. And let Trey sleep. I might even feed the young buck, but don't count on it.''

Slocum left the doctor grumbling about the inconvenience of keeping a patient overnight. He stepped into the main street, and noted how few men staggered along, going from one saloon to another. The town was dying, and for what?

Climbing tiredly into the saddle, Slocum headed out of town toward the Sleepy K. It felt almost as if he was riding home, he had made the trip so often. He arrived back about an hour after midnight, weaving in the saddle from lack of sleep. He and Trey had ridden out the previous day, and had ridden through Hell. Slocum's arms and legs twinged from the wounds he had received, but his muscles were the main source of downright agony.

He saw right away he wasn't going to get any sleep by the way Frank Kincannon came rushing out, waving his arms like some runaway windmill.

"Slocum, you got to help me."

"What is it, Mr. Kincannon?" Slocum went cold inside when he rode close enough to see the man's face. It had to be Elspeth.

"She's gone," was all Kincannon said, and Slocum knew his premonition had been dead on target.

"When? What happened?"

"The same as before. She . . . she just wandered off. She's not in her right mind. She doesn't know what she's doing when she's like this."

"When?" Slocum repeated.

"I don't know." The man was crying again, and wasn't a bit ashamed about it. "I just looked in on her and she was gone, then heard you riding in. She might be anywhere."

"Is she on foot?"

"Like before," Kincannon said, then looked shocked at what he had said.

Slocum whirled about, hand going for his six-shooter, when he heard a howling wolf.

"That came from north of here," he said to Kincannon. "Get mounted." Slocum didn't wait for Frank Kincannon. He put his heels to his tired horse's sides and got the animal trotting. Slocum had the sense that every instant mattered. The wolf call had sounded near. Elspeth wouldn't stand a chance against a solitary wolf—or a pack—if she was wandering in the dazed state that he had found her in after discovering Quinton Barnsley's corpse.

His horse balked at the pace he tried to set, forcing Slocum to slow, and finally to dismount. He grabbed his rifle and went ahead through a tangle of undergrowth on foot. His horse reared and its nostrils flared, warning Slocum it had detected something he hadn't.

A low grumbling growl alerted him. He swung up his rifle, ready to fire, as the bushes shook ahead of him.

A long snout poked through the thick bushes, but Slocum did not fire. Red eyes glared malevolently at him. And to the right another set appeared through dark shrubs. And more began appearing, ringing him in. His horse bolted and ran from the wolf pack, leaving Slocum to face a dozen wolves alone.

He lifted his rifle, wondering if killing one or two of the wolves would be enough to scare the rest off. Somehow, Slocum did not think it would.

His finger came back, then jerked in surprise when he heard an ear-shattering scream from behind him. The screech froze the wolves, and gave Slocum the chance to lever in another round and take better aim for a second shot. This one caused a large timber wolf to stagger and whimper, then limp off. Slocum started firing with an even rhythm, making every shot count.

The wolves snarled and began melting into shadow, running from their nemesis. When his rifle hammer fell on an empty chamber, Slocum noticed the wolf pack had disappeared entirely. He swung around in a full circle hunting for more of the gray killers. Slocum was alone in the forest, but the echo of the agonized scream still rang in his ears.

He tried to determine which direction it had come from, and decided to backtrack. It took him less than five minutes to find Frank Kincannon's body. The man lay on his back, eyes sightlessly staring up at the starry sky. His throat had been viciously ripped out.

Slocum knelt and closed the man's eyes. As he did so, he saw slight scuff marks in a patch of dirt beside the body. Slocum dropped to his belly and peered at the dirt, staring along a line parallel to the ground. He saw a faint track leading away into the forest, going off at an angle from where he had made his stand against the wolf pack.

Nowhere did Slocum see any paw prints he could identify as being made by a wolf.

Getting to his feet, Slocum patted his pockets, hunting for more ammunition for his Winchester. What spare ammo he had was in his saddlebags on a horse running frightened through the night. Slocum drew his Colt Navy and started in the direction of the tracks.

Ten minutes later Slocum heard noises ahead at the edge of the stand of trees. Then he heard the shrill laughter that he had heard before, but no wolf howl followed it. Picking up the pace, he blundered through the dark, and came out of the woods to see a ghostly figure stumbling along not twenty feet away.

"Elspeth!" he cried. She turned toward him, lost in the deep trance he had seen before. She held out her hands for him, took a step, and then collapsed.

13

Slocum rode with his arms around the swaying Elspeth Kincannon. She moaned now and then, but otherwise showed no sign of being alive. Bannock lay over the rise, but Slocum slowed, and then came to a complete halt before riding into town.

Elspeth needed a doctor's expert attention if she were to snap out of her trance. The paleness and the strange, vacant stare were so different from the bright, alive young woman he had seen so recently that Slocum knew something serious had to be wrong with her. And his guess at the source of Elspeth's malady lay in the medicine her mother gave her. If Dr. Talbot could tend her for a while, she might regain some semblance of her usual alert, active self.

Slocum wasn't sure what he would do if Talbot had no way of treating her. Returning Elspeth to her mother seemed a dangerous thing to do—and her father lay dead on his ranch, his throat ripped out by wolves. Or so it appeared to Slocum.

This time he found no blood on the woman to hint that she had been responsible for the gruesome death. Some blood stained the hem of her nightgown, but not the prodigious amount Slocum had found after he'd discovered Elspeth wandering near Quinton Barnsley's body. This time she did not have a mouthful of blood.

Her father's hot, spilled blood it would have been, Slocum reminded himself. It looked bad enough for Elspeth in her father's death, but the evidence was different now from what it had been in Barnsley's murder. Still, he had discovered Deputy Hines's torn vest and star in the woman's bedroom. Slocum wondered if the marshal would think him guilty also because he had buried her blood-soaked nightgown after Barnsley had been killed.

"Concealing evidence," Slocum muttered to himself. Not much of a crime, but enough to get him tossed into jail. If a lynch mob formed, they might want to string up anyone having anything to do with Barnsley's and Kincannon's murders. Slocum touched his neck, remembering what the bite of hemp felt like from one too many brushes with lynchings. He urged his horse forward, and stopped again to remain in shadows when he heard Pierre the Cajun bellowing out his message of hate.

"The *loup-garou*, she kill us all! The foreman of the Sleepy K is dead. Who might it have been who is so quick to slay?"

"Wolves!" shouted someone in the small crowd. Slocum wondered how Pierre had recruited so many for his harangue at this time of the night. Apparently, he had emptied the saloons with more news of the werewolf.

"No, no," Pierre said, dancing about and moving sinuously, reminding Slocum of some erect snake. "I say it is the *loup-garou*, she is responsible. You must find the woman who is a wolf and put an end to her killing."

Elspeth stirred in the circle of his arms. Slocum gentled his horse and tightened his grip on Elspeth. It wouldn't do right now to show himself—and Elspeth—to this crowd. Their mood was darkening by the minute as Pierre whipped them into a killing frenzy. Although he had not named the one he suspected of being the *loup-garou*, Pierre had little need to. Everyone in the throng seemed to know who he meant.

Elspeth Kincannon.

"She has killed her foreman, all bloody and terrible. She has killed a deputy. She has killed so many of the gallant men who work on her papa's ranch."

"Lynch her!" cried someone at the rear of the crowd.

"No, no, no! You cannot do that. To tie the rope around her neck is wrong. It would do nothing to kill her. She is *loup-garou*. She is the wolf. You must kill her with one of these!" Pierre held high one of his silver-painted bullets. The crowd surged closer, and bidding began for the purchase of the announced instrument of destruction for a she-wolf.

Slocum turned his horse and found dark back ways to reach Dr. Talbot's surgery. He jumped down, then let Elspeth fall into his arms. He carried her easily into the doctor's office. Talbot had been dozing at his desk, and sat up, eyes flying wide open. He fumbled a moment, found his glasses, and pulled them on.

"You looking for that young cowboy? He rode off—" Then he stopped, staring at Elspeth. "You do bring me the damnedest patients, Slocum. You lookin' to get a share of my fee?"

"Not this time, Doc," Slocum said, putting Elspeth down on the examining table. Her pulse was thready and her breathing ragged. The color had yet to return to her cheeks, but at least she wasn't stained red from her father's blood.

"What's wrong with the filly?" Talbot asked, peering down at Elspeth but not touching her. Slocum saw bloodstains on the doctor's hands. He had recently operated and had not yet cleaned himself. That mattered less than his ability to pull Elspeth from her stupor.

"You'll have to tell *me*. She wanders around in a trance, like a sleepwalker. Nothing wakes her up."

"Hmm, damned shame. Pretty young thing." Talbot looked up sharply at Slocum. "You get on out of here and let me look her over for damage, but you damn well get back here within an hour. She can't stay. I won't allow it!"

"The crowd?"

"Pierre's been beatin' those damn-fools into a frenzy for days. Why he chose Miss Kincannon is beyond me, but he did. Claims she is a wolf. Imagine that." Talbot snorted in contempt. The doctor rubbed his hands on his pants legs and began gathering examination equipment, laying it in a pan beside the table. Sprinkling carbolic acid on it caused noxious fumes to rise. Slocum stepped back to avoid them.

"I need to talk to the marshal," he said, "Be back as soon as I can."

"You don't go leavin' her now, damn you, Slocum. I will throw her to those human wolves, I will!" shouted Talbot. Slocum wasn't sure if the doctor meant it, but he just might. The sound from the crowd had turned ugly. In his day, he had heard more than his share of lynch mobs. Pierre fed their hatred and fear and raked in lots of money doing it, a deadly combination for Elspeth.

Slocum made his way down the street to the town jail. A pale yellow light shone under the door. Slocum rapped on the door. From inside came an immediate "Whatdya want?"

"I need to talk to you, Marshal," Slocum called. "It's about Frank Kincannon." He waited a few seconds before Jenks opened the door. Slocum was surprised that the marshal was dressed, had on his boots and gunbelt, and even carried a shotgun.

Seeing Slocum's reaction, Jenks said, "Can't sleep.

Figure I might as well be ready for whatever happens in Bannock.'' Jenks poked his head out and looked up and down the street. He paused a moment as he stared at Pierre and his followers. He spat, then pushed Slocum inside.

To one side of the small office stretched a cot. A small desk littered with papers made the room even more crowded. Slocum settled down in the single chair in front of the desk.

''What's this about Kincannon?'' Jenks demanded. From the tone of his voice, the marshal knew what was coming.

''He's dead,'' Slocum said. No need to sugarcoat it. ''I found his body not a mile from his ranch house.''

''Wolves?''

''Looked to be. I fought off a pack of timber wolves, then heard Mr. Kincannon cry out. By the time I got to him, he was dead.''

''Throat ripped out?''

Slocum nodded. And waited for the next question he knew the marshal would ask. He wasn't disappointed.

''Where was Miss Elspeth?''

''Twenty or thirty yards away,'' Slocum said. ''She was walking around in a trance, like she was sleepwalking. I don't think she saw anything.''

''She have blood on her?''

''Only on the hem of her nightgown,'' Slocum said. ''She must have walked right over her father's body, never seeing it.''

''So you say,'' Jenks said tiredly. ''You know what Pierre's been sayin' about her?''

Slocum heard the crowd's loud cheers and jeers. He nodded.

''Can't say I'm not inclined to go along with that,'' Jenks said. ''Her own mama told me she thought Miss

Elspeth might have had something to do with Quint's death.''

"Cora Kincannon said that?"

"Spoke with her and William Kincannon. That's exactly what she said. She was worried about her only daughter, and asked me what I could do to stop the killing.''

Slocum found this strange. Cora Kincannon had put Elspeth's neck in a noose asking questions like that.

"Who gets the Sleepy K now that Frank Kincannon's dead? His brother?"

"Will? Doubt it if Frank had anything to do with it, and he did. I'm sure he had a last will and testament drawn up. He and his brother have been on the outs for years. Never figured out what the bone of contention was, though.''

Slocum had a suspicion. Frank Kincannon was no man's fool. He might have learned his wife and brother were lovers behind his back.

"So who gets the Sleepy K?"

"If Will's not mentioned, I reckon it would be sold and the proceeds split between Elspeth and her ma.''

"That would make Elspeth very rich."

"Not so rich these days."

"It would make Cora Kincannon twice as rich if Elspeth didn't stand to inherit, wouldn't it?"

"You're paintin' that little lady with a mighty bold stroke, Slocum. Can't say I much like Cora Kincannon, never have, and I have a downright dislike for Will, but you make it sound as if they went to a lot of trouble to get possession of the Sleepy K.''

"What if Frank Kincannon was going to divorce his wife for infidelity?"

"The world's full of what-if-this and how-about-that, Slocum. I would need proof of such perfidy. Hate to say it, but the proof is going against Miss Elspeth right now.

Hell and damnation, I'm not sure Pierre hasn't convinced me she *is* one of them she-wolf critters he is always going on about.''

"Who would likely know these legal matters?" Slocum asked. "About the will and how Frank Kincannon wanted his estate handled?"

"Mrs. Kincannon, I'd say. Maybe his lawyer. That'd be old Seth Fenstermacher. Cranky and full of himself, but he does a good job when he gets down to anything legal.''

"I don't suppose this is a good time to see him," Slocum said, glancing at the Regulator clock balefully ticking off the seconds on the wall over the marshal's desk. It was almost five in the morning. Sunup would banish the tales of wolf-women and things that snarled in the night, at least until Pierre got up on his box again and started haranguing against Elspeth Kincannon.

"Seth's not inclined to see anybody at any time of the day," Jenks laughed. "But he might see you around noon, especially if you offered him lunch to go along with a little conversation.''

"Thanks, Marshal," Slocum said, knowing he couldn't stay in Bannock that long.

"Slocum, a word of advice. This ain't your fight.''

Slocum said nothing as he left. He remembered seeing Fenstermacher's law office when he rode into town. He walked quickly in that direction, finding the small clapboard shack about where he remembered it. Having no intention of asking for information and having a crotchety old galoot snap at him, Slocum chose a different route to the information he wanted.

The door was locked—but not for long. Slocum hit it twice with his shoulder, causing the hinges to pull free from the wood. He had to hang on to the door to keep it from falling inward. Guiding it around, he leaned it back, hoping no one outside would notice the strange angle and come to investigate.

He took a deep breath, inhaling the scent of aged, crumbling paper. Fenstermacher didn't seem to have an active practice, or if he did, he kept papers dating back for decades. Slocum cautiously prowled the office, wondering where he might find something as important as Frank Kincannon's will. He stopped in front of a large filing cabinet with a strong lock securing the top drawer. Rattling it futilely, he considered shooting the lock off.

As he drew his six-shooter, he froze. Sounds from outside alerted him to how bad an idea that would be. Slocum went to the door and peered around the edge. Pierre and his rabble came along singing some song in French that Slocum didn't understand, and he doubted any in the crowd did either.

"She is the source of our woe!" Pierre shouted. "She is the *loup-garou*! She is responsible for killing so many by tearing out their vulnerable throats!" Pierre grimaced and made a cutting motion with his finger across his dirty neck.

"A firing squad!" called someone in the crowd. "We get the Kincannon bitch and put her in front of a firing squad where everybody's got silver bullets loaded!"

Slocum lifted his six-gun and aimed it at Pierre. He didn't know if the Cajun was in cahoots with William and Cora Kincannon, or if he simply was taking advantage of a sad situation. He drew back when the swirl of the crowd took away his target. He could still hear Pierre, though.

"... keep her from town! Drive her away! She can only kill when she is under the moon spell!"

Slocum pressed himself against the wall, worrying that some of the crowd might see the door propped up against the wall and come to investigate. He didn't have a good story to give them. Worse, it wouldn't take Pierre but a few seconds to shift the blame for the wolf deaths from Elspeth to Slocum.

"She stays on her ranch where she is safe, but others around her are not so safe!" Pierre said. "The *loup-garou*, she can turn against her own flesh and blood! Who knows the next victim?"

Slocum seethed. It might be coincidence, but it sounded as if Pierre knew Frank Kincannon was dead and was pointing the blame straight at Elspeth. Quinton Barnsley had done the fetching and toting for Mrs. Kincannon. It didn't take much imagination to see how Pierre could be doing the same now, closing the case against Elspeth with words rather than laudanum.

The crowd pressed through a small door into a saloon down the street. Their boisterous cries for blood echoed faintly to Slocum, telling him time was running out for Elspeth Kincannon. He had to find out what William Kincannon stood to gain.

William *and* Cora.

Turning back to the file cabinet, he lifted his six-shooter and started to blow off the lock. Then good sense hit him. If he left behind evidence of tampering, William Kincannon might get the will overturned in court. The door might be explained away, but a blown-off lock was evidence someone had poked around in the files.

"The marshal said Fenstermacher was an old man," Slocum said out loud. "Old men might get forgetful. An old man might leave the key to his files nearby." Slocum holstered his Colt and began looking for a key. He found it a few minutes later in the unlocked top desk drawer.

The lock yielded easily, and he drew out the contents of the cabinet, laying the stack of papers on the lawyer's desk. It took several minutes to leaf through the documents, but he soon came to Frank Kincannon's sworn and signed will.

Slocum wasn't sure what a lot of the legal maundering meant, but he read enough to cause his eyebrows to rise in surprise. It came as no surprise that Frank had not liked his brother William overmuch. He tolerated him, but thought he was a wastrel and a fool, unable to handle money properly.

As such, William Kincannon had been cut out of the inheritance entirely. What did surprise Slocum was the revelation that Cora Kincannon was not Frank's first wife. His first wife, Sarah, had died in childbirth, giving life to Elspeth. A long maudlin paragraph detailed Kincannon's love for Sarah for giving him such a lovely, loving daughter.

"Second wife," he said. "And she's not Elspeth's mother. She is her stepmother."

That brought a great deal into focus for him. Frank Kincannon had wanted his daughter to benefit in case of his death, not his second wife. Slocum read enough of the words to guess Frank Kincannon had known for some time of his wife's infidelity with his brother.

Tucked in with the will was another document, legally drawn but unsigned. It was a petition for a divorce.

"So Frank *was* divorcing Cora, cutting her out entirely, like he already had his brother. That leaves Elspeth as his sole heir. Unless she isn't around to collect."

Without the divorce final, and with Elspeth dead or in jail, Cora stood to inherit the Sleepy K.

"Not too bad. She's free of a husband she doesn't love and a stepdaughter she really doesn't care for—and she's rich." Slocum had discovered plenty of motive for Cora Kincannon to make it appear Elspeth was a killer, but he still had to prove it.

That might not be too easy because time was running out. Pierre and his *loup-garou* hunters might see that it ran out completely if they got wind of Elspeth being in town.

14

Dr. Talbot looked up sharply when Slocum came in. The doctor seemed shaky, and sweat beaded his forehead. He pushed away from his desk and steadied himself, one hand against a wall and the other on the back of the desk chair.

"You took your time, damn you," Talbot snapped. He rubbed his hands against his pants legs, and then swung around to stare intently at Elspeth. "I can't look after her much longer. They are everywhere in this town. Damned fools, all of them, mumbling about matters they don't know jackshit about. Pierre is the worst of the bunch, inciting them to violence like he is. Wish I'd never crossed paths with that son of a bitch. There ought to be a law."

"There probably is," Slocum said. He went to the examining table. Elspeth seemed to be sleeping peacefully now. The drawn look had faded from her features, and a spot of color had returned to her checks.

"What was wrong with her?"

"Can't say for certain," Talbot said. "From the way her pupils were contracted, she might have taken too much laudanum."

"Laudanum?" Slocum sucked in his breath and held it. Barnsley had been supplying Cora Kincannon with the tincture of opium. Cora had slipped it into Elspeth's food or water, telling her it was medicine, perhaps at first not even telling her she was administering it. Slocum released his breath.

"You know how dangerous laudanum is, don't you?" Talbot asked.

"I know," Slocum said. He had seen those addicted to opium and what the drug did to them. "Is there anything that can help get it out of her body?"

"Time," Dr. Talbot said, frowning as he thought on it, as if this were a deeply philosophical subject to him. "Don't let her take any more. Her memory's going to be spotty, if she can remember anything at all. I don't know that much about the other effects, but it's not too damned good."

"Doc," Slocum said, "Frank Kincannon's been murdered. Looks like a wolf—or wolves. Elspeth was wandering nearby," He paused while Talbot frowned again. "I got to ask you a question. Could Elspeth kill someone while under the influence of the laudanum?"

"Maybe, but I doubt it. She wanders around in a daze and can't concentrate. Her emotions are muted, and I doubt she even sees too well. And dammit, look at how frail she is! The drug would make her weaker, not stronger." Dr. Talbot tipped his head a little and peered at Slocum. "You think they gave Miss Elspeth the drug to cover their own damned guilt in the killing?"

Talbot didn't bother supplying who he thought "they" were. Both he and Slocum were following the same thread of logic to the identical conclusion.

"I don't want to take her back to the Sleepy K," Slocum said, "not with Cora Kincannon running it now."

"You figure she's the one? Not Will?" The doctor

stared at Slocum, his eyes fathomless brown pools. Slocum blinked as he felt himself being pulled down into them.

"Let's say I checked some legal papers. Cora is Frank Kincannon's second wife. But the Sleepy K is all Elspeth's, unless she's dead. Then it ought to go to Cora."

"So Frank shut his brother out. That explains the rumors I've heard for months about Cora and Will. You figure they killed Frank?"

Slocum remembered how Kincannon's throat had been ripped out, making it seem a wolf had been at work. How many others had been killed? Whatever the number, it had been too many. William and Cora Kincannon had slaughtered anyone getting in their way.

"You look like someone just poked you," Talbot said. "What else is there?"

"Just a guess," Slocum said. Before he could elaborate, he heard a loud roar from the crowd outside in the street. Slocum went to the surgery door and opened it a few inches.

"What's going on?" Talbot asked.

"Can't rightly tell," Slocum said, "but there are a powerful lot of men complaining about it. Wait here. I'll be right back." He slipped out of the doctor's office, ignoring Talbot's protests. He walked briskly to the edge of the crowd. From his vantage point he could see two horses and the top of Marshal Jenks's head. Otherwise, the surging crowd blocked his view.

"What's going on?" he asked a man crowding next to him.

"Found the *loup-garou*," the drunken man said. "Need to string 'er up! Stop the killin' now!"

Slocum pushed through the crowd until he got a better view. He tensed, his hand going to his holstered Colt Navy when he saw Cora Kincannon and her brother-in-law talking with Marshal Jenks. Cora was waving her hands around wildly and sounded distraught, but Slocum saw the steely glint in her eye. She was playacting.

"Dead, I tell you, Marshal. She killed him. *Elspeth killed my husband!*"

"Heard a report on this already, Mrs. Kincannon. Haven't had time to investigate."

"Who told you?" demanded William Kincannon. "Not Elspeth. She killed her own father. She's a dangerous woman and has to be caught immediately."

"Not her," Jenks said. From the corner of his eye he saw Slocum. He turned away, ignoring the source of information about Kincannon's death. For that Slocum thanked him silently.

"We saw her do it," said Cora. "She . . . she seemed to become an animal. She ripped his throat out with her teeth!" Cora sobbed. "I've never seen anything so awful, so brutal. She's more animal than human!"

"*Loup-garou!*" the crowd chanted. Slocum saw the Cajun at the back, softly urging those around him to join in. Between the Kincannons and Pierre, they had the crowd riled up against Elspeth, who'd been condemned and sentenced to swing from the tallest tree they could find.

"I need to look at the body," Jenks said. "If the evidence goes against your daughter, she'll stand trial for murder. Don't matter if it was her pa or some stranger what died. If Miss Elspeth is guilty, she'll pay the price demanded by the law." Jenks spoke with a coldness in his voice intended to stifle dissent in the crowd. It failed.

"Make her pay the price!" cried Pierre. "She is the evil one! Make her pay now!"

"Where is she?" asked William Kincannon of the marshal. "Are you hiding her out?"

"What are you accusing me of?" growled Jenks. "I haven't seen hide nor hair of her in days."

The unfortunate phrase set off the crowd again.

"Loup-garou!" they shouted. "She's a wolf. Kill her 'fore she kills again!"

"There was Barnsley!" someone called out from the far side of the crowd. "And nobody ever found Hines's body! Maybe she done et him! Maybe she et both of 'em!"

Slocum began moving away, knowing the mood was turning against anyone the least bit sympathetic to Elspeth Kincannon. If Cora spotted him, she would have the crowd tear him to pieces. Slocum had little trouble getting away from the center of the storm because William Kincannon mounted his horse and shouted, "Search the town for her! She must be around somewhere! She left the Sleepy K to kill her pa! If she is a *loup-garou,* she has a den around here somewhere!"

Slocum didn't follow the logic, but it hardly mattered to the crowd. It gave them something to do other than stand and chant.

They moved down the street heading for the hotel. Slocum backed off, then dashed for the doctor's office. He rattled the handle until Talbot unlocked the door and let him inside.

"They're hunting for her. Cora and Will have them stirred up and ready to kill Elspeth for killing her pa."

"She didn't do it," Talbot said flatly.

"We know that. They don't. Cora wants Elspeth dead so she can take over the Sleepy K."

"I'd be mighty uneasy about sleeping with that woman if I were Will Kincannon," observed Talbot. "She got rid of one husband, and would kill her stepdaughter to get control of the ranch. No telling what she'd do to another man if he crossed her."

"Does one snake worry about the others in its den?" Slocum asked. He shook Elspeth. The woman moaned, and tried to roll onto her side.

"Lemme sleep. So tired," she said.

"Is there anything you can do to get her awake?"

"Reckon so," Talbot said. He went to her, reached down, and pinched her earlobe. The woman's eyes shot wide open, and she let out a screech that was decidedly wolflike as she grabbed for the damaged lobe.

"You and Slocum have to get the hell out," Talbot said. "Damned if it is safe, even in my office."

"Dr. Talbot," Elspeth said, as if recognizing where she was for the first time. "What are you doing here?" She sat up and looked around. Bewilderment etched itself onto her fine features. "I don't understand what's going on." The plaintive plea in her voice moved Slocum.

"I'll tell you later," Slocum said, "Right now, we have to go. Fast, Elspeth, fast."

"Where are you heading?" asked Talbot. Then he held up his hand. "Wait, don't tell me. I can't reveal what I damned well don't know."

"I'll explain everything, but you have to walk," Slocum told her. "We have to dodge a lynch mob hunting for you."

"A lynch mob? Me? John, I—" He clamped his hand over her mouth to silence her. Outside the doctor's office came loud calls from a dozen men. A hard rapping on the door echoed throughout the surgery.

Talbot pointed toward the back way. Slocum grabbed Elspeth and shoved her ahead of him. He dropped curtains behind him, and hesitated long enough to see Talbot open the door. Slocum was surprised at the older man's strength as he held back three burly cowboys determined to search his office.

"You shot up or you got some damned sickness rotting away your innards, then I see you," Talbot said. "Otherwise, I don't want to clean the place from you tracking in so much mud." They tried to force their way in again, and again Talbot easily shoved them back. Slo-

cum didn't stay to see anymore. He joined Elspeth in
the alley behind the doctor's office.

"Where are we going? Back to the Sleepy K?" she
asked, confused at the rush of events.

"No," was all he had time to say. He guided her
down the alley, and finally reached a burned-out building at the edge of town. The walls had been hacked off
or burned down to shoulder-level. The acrid smell from
the recent fire stung his nostrils, but Slocum still pushed
Elspeth down into a pile of ash, half covering her.

"They might not find us here," he said.

"John, what is going on?" she demanded.

"You seem to have most of the drug out of your
body," he said, wondering how much he could tell her
without having her go to pieces. Her father was dead,
but did she know? Really know?

He told her straight out. As he had when reporting
Frank Kincannon's murder to the marshal, Slocum saw
no need to soften the blow now to Elspeth. The sooner
she realized how bad her situation was, the sooner they
could start finding a way out of it.

"Dead? My papa's dead?" Her eyes went wide and
tears welled. Her face took on the ghostly pallor again,
but Slocum saw the vein pulsing at her temple. This
wasn't the bloodless look she'd had before when she
was drugged. This was shock.

Elspeth buried her face in Slocum's shoulder and
sobbed uncontrollably. Slocum let her get out her feel-
ings before he added the rest of the bad news to her
already heaping plate.

"Your uncle and stepmother both accuse you of killing him."

"Me? But I didn't—" She pulled back and stared at
Slocum. "Stepmother? What do you mean?"

"Cora Kincannon is your father's second wife. Your
real mother died giving birth to you," Slocum said.

Elspeth wobbled a little and fell back into the ashes. For a few seconds Slocum thought she would faint, but she was made of sterner stuff. Her lips moved as if she sought the right words. Then she took a deep breath and got control of her rampaging emotions. Seldom had he seen a woman, have more bad heaped on her—or anyone, man or woman—and show such courage dealing with it.

"What can we do? If they are accusing me, we have to find who is really responsible. There's no way I can ever prove myself innocent. I have to show who is really guilty."

"It looked like a wolf," Slocum said.

"Then the marshal will see that and—"

"They've built quite a case for you being one of the Cajun's *loup-garous*. They told Jenks you turned into a wolf, killed your pa, then ran off. With so many others being killed by the wolf pack, they might stick you with those murders too."

"You keep saying murders. If wolves killed them all, that's not murder."

"I don't think a wolf killed your father. Or Barnsley. Or Deputy Hines, and maybe not most of the others. It's unusual, even with a rabid wolf pack, for an animal to stalk a human. We're too cranky and dangerous, and I suppose we taste bad."

"Someone's responsible for all the killing?"

"There's been a fair amount of rustling going on. And I think your stepmother's responsible for running off the owners of the ranches adjacent to the Sleepy K."

"I can't believe she's not my mother. How do you know?"

Slocum didn't want to go into his breaking and entering so he could read private files in the lawyer's office.

"I've found out, and I think most folks will believe it, if they aren't caught up in the fear of a werewolf."

"How superstitious can people get?" she wondered. Elspeth moved closer to Slocum and clung to him for support. Again he felt the hot tears staining his shirt, but this time Elspeth did not sob.

"We can't stay here," he said, "I saw an abandoned house a ways down the road. We might hide out there for a while, until the crowd gets tired and breaks up. Not even Pierre can keep them het up for days on end."

"All right," Elspeth said softly. She kept pace with Slocum, in spite of his long, rapid strides. It was getting near dawn, and he didn't want to be seen.

"There it is," he said. "When folks started leaving Bannock, this is one they just walked away from." He pushed open the balky door and peered inside, wary of a trap. His caution proved needless. A table and two chairs dominated the middle of the single room, and a largish bed on the far side provided the only other furniture.

"Not my idea of home, but it'll do. Are all hideouts this sparse?" she asked.

"Why ask me?"

"You have the look of a man who is dangerous, John. And a dangerous man has to stay on the run. Do you hide out in places like this often?"

"Not too often," he said, sitting beside her on the straw-filled mattress. "Usually they're worse."

She smiled at this. Then the smile faded. Their eyes locked. She reached out tentatively, her hand brushing across his cheek. Elspeth moved closer and her eyes closed. She kissed him softly on the lips, then hugged him stronger than a bear ever could.

Elspeth had lost everything this night. Her father was murdered, and the woman she had thought her mother all her life had proved to be false. Slocum wasn't about to deny her what might be her only anchor to sanity.

They sank back to the bed, passionately wrestling.

The ropes under the straw mattress creaked, and it flattened in places. Slocum hardly noticed the discomfort. Elspeth unbuttoned his jeans and tugged eagerly at the stiff shaft jutting from his groin.

"So hard, and all for me," she said softly. Stroking up and down the length, she made Slocum come even more alive. To repay her, his hands sought out all the right places on her body, touching sensitive breasts, and finally pushing aside the thick curtains of her skirt to reveal the fleecy triangle nestled between her legs.

"Oh!" she cried in a small voice as his finger entered her. She kept stroking up and down his length, and he began moving his finger in and out of her. For a while this was enough. Then their passions reached the point where both needed more.

Mouths locked together, they kissed deeply. Slocum's tongue invaded her mouth and dueled with her darting pink tongue before retreating. He felt his bare chest crushing down into her breasts. Twin nubs hardened at the crests of her tits and poked passionately into him.

"Yes, John, now, do it now. I need to forget everything. Make me forget. Make love to me!"

Her knees lifted on either side of his body as he positioned himself. Her grip around him was like a beacon in the night. She drew him directly to the moist target both wanted to hit dead center. His hips moved slightly, following the direction dictated by her hand. The tip of his manhood brushed across the fleecy mat between her thighs, then sank far up into her most intimate recess.

Elspeth shrieked at the sudden intrusion. Then she brought her hips up off the bed and began grinding them down around him, to take even more of his meaty shaft into her.

Slocum reveled in the feel of tight female flesh all around him. Then he had to move. Withdrawing slowly, he relished every tingle and twitch of his organ. Then he slid fully back into her. This ignited both of their desires so there was no turning back.

Faster and faster he stroked, turning into a human piston. Elspeth gasped and moaned and contributed all she could to the mutual lovemaking. Slocum wasn't sure how long it lasted, but it wasn't long enough.

He spilled his seed, and she shuddered as intense emotion racked her body. Then they both sank to the thin mattress and held one another.

For Elspeth, this was what she needed. For Slocum, it was pure torture. He had wasted time when Frank Kincannon's real killers were out agitating against Elspeth. In time the woman drifted to sleep, allowing Slocum to climb from the bed and dress.

As he strapped on his six-gun, he looked down at her while she slept fitfully.

"They're not going to get away with it, I promise you that much," he said aloud. He found a piece of charcoal in the fireplace and wrote a short note to her on the tabletop. Then he went out to get evidence that would clear Elspeth Kincannon of murder.

And of being a *loup-garou.*

15

Slocum figured Elspeth would stay put unless the crowd came for her. He had a world of evidence to collect if he wanted to clear her of the foul cloud of suspicion Pierre—and William and Cora Kincannon—had blown around her. He thought everything was tied together, and one thread would pull lose the entire garment of lies.

He headed for where his horse was tethered. As he made his way down Bannock's main street, Slocum noticed small knots of armed men skulking about. He didn't bother asking what they were doing. They hunted *loup-garou*.

As he passed the apothecary shop, he turned and went inside. A small, mousy man looked up over the tops of thick glasses. He was working hard at grinding a white powder with mortar and pestle.

"How can I help you?" he asked in a nasal voice.

Slocum scratched his head slowly and looked pensive, as if he was wrestling with something beyond his experience. "I'm the new foreman out at the Sleepy K, and Miz Kincannon sent me in to buy some more of the medicine. I'm not real sure what it was she was talking about." He tried to look as confused as he could.

"Heard about poor Quint. Good man. Hell of a way to die, getting your throat savaged by wolves." He peered at Slocum for a moment, as if coming to a decision. "I reckon Mrs. Kincannon wants more of the medicine for her daughter." The man pushed the glasses up on his nose, turned, and slowly worked his way down a shelf loaded with envelopes filled with various drugs. The pharmacist snatched up one and tossed it onto the counter. "This will fix Miss Elspeth right up."

"What is it?" Slocum asked, picking it up and peering at the white powder inside.

"Same as always," the pharmacist said coldly. "That'll be a dollar."

"Right here," Slocum said, fumbling in his shirt pocket and pulling out a greenback.

"Don't you go sniffin' that stuff. It's not good for you, if you don't need it."

"Sniff it?" Slocum closed the envelope and pushed it into his pocket. "Wouldn't dream of doing a thing like that."

This satisfied the pharmacist.

"No, sir," Slocum said. "Sniffing laudanum can be downright dangerous, can't it?"

"You said it," the pharmacist said, not even looking up from his grinding.

Slocum left, his suspicions confirmed. Cora Kincannon had been drugging her daughter until she wandered about mindlessly. In that condition, Elspeth might be convinced she had done something terrible—or might be purposely maneuvered into the vicinity of a death. Slocum's image of her with Barnsley's blood still dribbling from her lips made him shiver.

William and Cora had gone to a great deal of trouble to make it look as if Elspeth was a demented killer capable of killing her own father.

Slocum found his horse, mounted, and rode from

town. William and Cora didn't seem to be anywhere around. They might be holed up somewhere, or they might have ridden back to the Sleepy K. Either way was fine with Slocum. If he found them at the ranch, he could force their hand. He knew about the laudanum. If they weren't there, he could hunt for more evidence that would prove Elspeth's innocence.

The only problem he saw was that legal evidence, facts given in court, might never be allowed in front of a lynch mob. Pierre had worked up the town to the point they'd kill anyone they suspected of being a *loup-garou.*

Slocum considered riding past the abandoned house to be sure Elspeth was still there. He ought to have made it clear to her what his plans were, but he now avoided the house in case anyone was watching him. Besides, Slocum knew Elspeth would have insisted on coming with him. That would never do with everyone in the territory looking for a werewolf.

He rode out of town and picked up the pace, wanting to finish off the hunt for evidence as quick as he could. Arriving at the Sleepy K, he went directly to the ranch house. Rather than knock, Slocum pushed open the door and listened intently for any sound inside. He regretted not locating William and Cora Kincannon before barging in. They were probably still in town inciting the crowds gathered by the Cajun against Elspeth. Slocum didn't cotton much to poking around in the house only to get backshot by one of them.

"Anyone here?" he called. He stepped into the house and closed the door when he got no answer. A quick search of the large house assured him he was alone. Slocum felt like a thief as he poked around, looking for something he wouldn't recognize until he saw it.

Twenty minutes of searching revealed nothing he could use as evidence against William and Cora. Then he found the family bible. It lay on a table, pushed to one side. Dust around it had been disturbed, showing it had been moved recently.

Slocum picked up the large book, and noted it had seen better days. Most of the pages were stuck together.

"Someone dropped it in water," he said to himself. Then he saw a few pages at the back had been carefully pried apart. Setting the book down, he read the pages that had already attracted someone's attention.

"The Kincannon curse?" he said aloud, trying to keep from laughing. But his merriment faded as he read how every other generation of Kincannon women had been afflicted. "For eighty years, their own families thought they were *loup-garous*," he said aloud, shaking his head in amazement. The terse biographies were bleak. Anyone reading this might have gotten the idea to make Elspeth look like a *loup-garou*, and then claim it was only the Kincannon curse reasserting itself.

Slocum spun, hand going for his six-shooter, when he heard the front door opening. He relaxed when he saw Trey standing in the doorway.

"It's me, Slocum. I wondered if Mrs. Kincannon had come back from town. I worried she might not have found Miss Elspeth."

"She hasn't found her," Slocum said, not wanting to burden the young cowboy with information he didn't need. He glanced a final time at the pages describing Kincannon lycanthropy.

"I'm feeling better," Trey said. "Got back here on my own. Doc Talbot's a strange bird." He moved his arm in a wide circle, grimaced a little, and then smiled. "I've been laying on that arm to rest my leg in just the right position. Arm cramped up something fierce and hurts worse than the leg."

"You up for riding?" Slocum asked.

"Back to catch the rustlers?" Trey asked. An eagerness came to his tone now, telling he wanted to even the score.

"Fetch your hogleg, saddle up, and we can ride. I'm getting an idea who might be behind the rustling."

Trey turned, hesitated, then faced Slocum. "I heard some rumors back in town," Trey said. "Might not mean spit, but I wonder."

"What were they?" Slocum asked.

"I don't want to seem disloyal," Trey started. "Hell, Slocum, I heard it's William Kincannon who's been buying up the ranches around here. Not direct-like, but doing it sneaky through some law company in Helena. Why he'd want to hide what he's doing makes me think that, well, it sure looks suspicious."

"Like William Kincannon is rustling cattle, then moving them out on the railroad spur?"

"Something like that." Trey seemed uncomfortable at the accusation.

"I think that's only part of what's happening. There was a wolf pack preying on the cattle, and maybe even a man or two, but I think Kincannon's the one responsible for killing most of the men who've died."

"To cover his own tracks, he made it look like wolves did the murdering?"

"Worse than that," Slocum said, closing the bible. "Worse than that."

Slocum saw how Trey favored his injured leg. The man wasn't fully healed. Considering how recently he had been wounded, slocum wasn't surprised. He hoped the tender leg wouldn't keep Trey from acting when he had to. This time Slocum knew what he was up against, and wanted to end the rustlers' careers once and for all.

Then he would let the marshal sort out the problems, make the accusations, bring the charges. With full-scale rustling to distract the townspeople, no one might notice

Pierre and his tall tales about *loup-garou* and how they'd thought Elspeth was one.

Stealing cattle was a lot more concrete than thinking girls into animals and ran around in the night ripping out the throats of men twice their size and strength.

"We don't hit them straight on," Slocum told Trey. "Get evidence, then settle scores."

"You mean we hightail it if the going gets too tough?" Trey sounded outraged at such cowardice.

"Something like that. We can't fight an army. George Pickett proved that. We do what we can, we get out, and let the marshal finish the battle, if it comes to that."

"Galls me thinking we might have to turn tail," Trey grumbled.

"We didn't do so good the first time. Now we know what to expect. That gives us an advantage, but if we don't use it fast, we had better run even faster."

"All right," Trey said, still not happy with the plan.

They rode through the saddleback and into the valley again. This time Slocum had no reason to follow the tracks from rustled cattle. He silently indicated that he and Trey ought to skirt the broad grassy meadow and head directly for the railroad spur. If there were rustlers around, that was where they would most likely congregate.

"I hear something," Trey said. Slocum had already heard the low voices and smelled the horses. He motioned for the cowboy to dismount. They tethered their horses near a small stream and advanced on foot, rifles ready.

Slocum flopped onto his belly when he saw movement ahead. Trey followed him to the ground. The young cowboy clenched his rifle stock so hard, his hands shook.

"Relax," Slocum advised. The cowboy did his best

to obey. Only when Slocum thought Trey wasn't likely to accidentally trigger a round did he motion for them to advance.

Two men crouched by a fire, a pot of coffee boiling. One spat out the coffee dregs and dashed the grounds from his cup into the dirt.

"You make piss-poor coffee."

"Boil your own," the second rustler said amiably.

"When's the boss getting here?"

"Soon, in an hour, next year, how should I know?" The second man sipped at the coffee as if it was the finest he had ever tasted. Slocum saw the man's secret ingredient. The rustler poured a stiff slug of bourbon into the cup before drinking more.

"We can't keep on rustling here. The marshal's wise to us, and that cowboy we ran off—what was his name?"

"Slocum," said the second man, savoring a mouthful of the coffee. "He's playing right into the boss's hand. We'll be out of here before you know it."

"We done stole every beef worth its salt. Why should we stick around any longer?"

"The boss says so, that's why. He bought two more ranches this past week. Two more to go and he owns a spread that'll make the King look like a sodbuster's hundred-sixty acres."

"What's he know? He's not running the operation. Mrs. Kincannon is. You can tell by the way he jumps every time she snaps her fingers."

"What difference does it make who's calling the shots?" asked the more contented rustler. He finished his coffee in a rush, then poured more, adding his special flavoring.

"Taking orders from a woman galls me."

"She's a rich widow, Lucas," said the second rustler, smiling a bit. "She might take a fancy to you. Marry her, and you can end up with a million acres of Montana.''

''I wouldn't want to get that close to her daughter. She's a *loup-garou*, you know. That Cajun bastard in town said so.''

''You don't believe that drivel, do you?'' He drank again, then held his tin cup high as if studying its contents.

''We done stole all the beeves around here. What difference does it make now?''

''I think we have other trouble,'' the second rustler said. The tone of his voice put Slocum on edge. He levered a round into the chamber of his Winchester at the same time the rustler dropped his cup and spun over flat on his belly, six-shooter leveled and firing.

''They spotted us!'' cried Trey, getting a face full of dirt and stone kicked up in front of him by the slug.

Slocum squeezed the rifle trigger and brought down the first, complaining rustler. Trey was slower, and had more to contend with. He fired, but missed. Slocum turned his rifle on the second rustler, and also missed the second man, who had spotted them in the reflection in his tin cup. This gave their target the chance to grab wildly for his rifle and sprint for cover behind the cord of wood meant to fuel the boiler of the locomotive that took the stolen beeves down the line.

''He's out of my line of fire, Slocum,'' Trey said. ''I'll circle him so we can get him in a cross fire.''

Slocum let him go, keeping the rustler pinned down with withering fire. Slocum began worrying about his ammo supply. He had expected a hard-fought battle, but not one requiring hundreds of rounds to be fired. When he'd left his horse and the saddlebags dangling over its rump, he had thrust only a single box of shells into his pocket.

He reloaded now, counting what he had left. It hadn't

even been a full box. He had twenty rifle rounds remaining, plus those in his Colt Navy.

It might be enough going against a solitary outlaw. It would have to be.

Slocum saw Trey moving to higher ground. The young cowboy got into position, but did not open fire. "What's wrong?" Slocum shouted.

"We got company on the way," Trey responded.

This galvanized the rustler into action. He got his feet under him and sprinted for the tracks. Both Slocum and Trey tried to bring him down, but the man moved fast, dodged, and got lucky. Slocum was sure he came close a couple times, but never winged the running outlaw.

"Here, here, we're being attacked!" the rustler shouted as he ran along the tracks in the direction of the approaching train. The locomotive applied its brakes, sending foot-long sparks shooting out from the steel wheels. The pungent odor of hot metal blew into Slocum's face, telling him he and Trey didn't have much time left.

"Get on out!" Slocum shouted to his companion. "We can't stand them all off!"

"Cattle, Slocum! Behind me down the hill are a hundred head of cattle! They look to have the Rolling J brand on them! This herd's been rustled from Colonel Jerome! Get him on our side and—"

"Trey!" Slocum's warning came too late. The cowboy had been too engrossed in his discovery of newly stolen cattle to see how a dozen men were piling from the train, rifles and shotguns ready.

Slocum wasn't sure it was William Kincannon who pulled the trigger that brought down Trey, but it might have been. The man stood half a head taller than any of the rustlers around him. And the way his lips curled in a self-satisfied grin told Slocum the man *thought* he had killed Trey.

That seemed good enough to condemn the man. Slocum started firing, and drew their fire from the fallen man on the hilltop.

"Slocum!" bellowed Kincannon. "It's Slocum! Kill the son of a bitch! A hundred-dollar reward for the man who kills Slocum!"

Muzzles of a dozen killers' rifles swung in his direction. Slocum was torn. He didn't like leaving a fallen comrade, but Trey wasn't moving. The young cowboy lay with his arms flung out and his face squarely in the dirt. Slocum couldn't tell from this distance, but it didn't seem that Trey was breathing.

He sure as hell wasn't moving—and Slocum could never carry him to safety. Puffs of dirt began kicking up all around Slocum's feet, warning him of imminent death unless *he* moved. He backed off, firing with a steady, deadly accuracy that caused two of the rustlers to grab injured parts of their anatomy. But he had no time to reload. At this range, his six-gun wasn't going to be effective.

Hating it, but knowing he had no other choice, Slocum got to his feet and ran like the hounds of Hades nipped at his heels. From the way the air filled with death-giving lead, he knew that he wasn't far wrong in his appraisal.

16

Slocum got to where he and Trey had tethered their horses. He took both horses, intending to ride Trey's until the animal faltered under him, then switch to his own. Outrunning the rustlers might not be as easy as it had before. Then they had simply retreated. Now, with William Kincannon urging them on, they were out for blood.

Slocum's blood.

Behind him Slocum heard the pounding of half-a-dozen horses. Glancing behind, he took in the scene and cursed. Kincannon had had the horses with him on the train, and all were fresh.

"Come on, boy," Slocum grated into the horse's ear. Trey had trained his horse well. It put down its head and galloped hard for almost a mile before tiring. Slocum slowed a mite and checked the pursuit. Kincannon led the pack of howling, wildly gesturing outlaws. For a hundred dollars, any of those men would have slit his own grandmother's throat. Getting caught by them meant death—and it wasn't likely to be an easy one.

Slocum could think of a half-dozen ways of killing a man to make it look as if a wolf had done the deed. He was certain Kincannon had thought up several more. One would be used on Slocum, then Elspeth would be blamed. Even if he didn't want to save his own precious hide, getting Elspeth into even deeper trouble didn't sit well with Slocum.

Trey's horse began to stumble. Slocum jumped off onto his own, and an instant later, the horse he'd just left stuck a foot down a gopher hole. The snapping leg sounded like a gunshot. The horse whinnied in pain and went down, white bone thrusting through bloody flesh on its right front leg.

Slocum wished he had time to put the animal out of its misery. He wished Kincannon would do it. He wished to hell he had not shoved his head into the steely jaws of such a trap.

His sturdy pony valiantly kept up the pace, and Kincannon's gang slowly fell farther and farther back. By the time Slocum had to rest his horse or have it drop dead under him, he had far out-legged the pursuing rustlers.

"Take it easy," Slocum said, dismounting and patting the horse's neck. He let the horse drink greedily from a stream before pulling it away. One huge brown eye turned accusingly on him. "Sorry about that. Don't want you to take on a bloat."

The horse did not care. Slocum waited a few minutes, then let the horse drink a bit more. Then he got into the saddle and headed straight for town. He knew more than he had when he left, but none of the evidence was much good. It was a case of his word against William Kincannon's. But the more Slocum learned of the cattle rustlers and the way Cora Kincannon had drugged her stepdaughter, the more of a case he could make against William and Cora.

Sooner or later he would accumulate enough to make

even the most skeptical marshal and judge and jury believe.

First, he had to fetch Elspeth. Slocum circled Bannock and came in from a direction intended to confuse anyone on his trail. He quickly discovered it was all in vain.

Elspeth Kincannon was gone.

Slocum looked for tracks, and saw nothing to hint she had been taken by a mob. But there weren't tracks of any other kind he could decipher either. His heart hammered, and then slowed as he thought about what he might do. If Cora or William Kincannon had taken her, she might be dead by now. They would have turned her over to the Cajun and his lynch mob so their hands would be clean of Elspeth's death.

"Marshal Jenks," Slocum said to himself reluctantly. He tugged on the reins and got his tired horse moving. He had to see the marshal anyway. If he kept heaping enough bits and pieces of evidence on the marshal's doorstep, sooner or later Jenks would respond to it.

But Slocum felt as if he had been dealt a pair of deuces and everyone else in the game had a full house.

No loud shouts laden with blood lust filled the air as he rode directly to the marshal's office. The Bannock hoosegow seemed no different from when he had been there before—only hours ago, but seemingly decades earlier. So much had happened. Too much for Slocum to appreciate it.

He dismounted and went inside, startling the marshal. The man's hands grabbed at the sawed-off scattergun on the desk. Jenks didn't lower it when Slocum closed the door behind him.

"Mighty jumpy, aren't you, Marshal?" Slocum asked.

"You get on out of here. I don't want anyone in this jailhouse."

"Why not? I've got evidence of—"

."Get the hell out, Slocum, or I'll ventilate that worthless hide of yours."

Before Slocum could say a word, he heard a plaintive cry from the cells in back.

"John! Get me out!"

"Elspeth!" he shouted, then froze in his tracks. Jenks drew back both hammers on the shotgun. At this range, Slocum's belly would be nothing more than bloody mist.

"I'm keepin' her from talkin' to anyone else," Jenks said. "That means you too, Slocum."

"How'd you get her?"

"Happenstance," Jenks said, his face twisted into a sour expression. "I was riding around town when I caught sight of her in an abandoned house on the edge of town. But I reckon you know which one I mean, don't you, Slocum?"

"I've got more evidence on the rustlers. William Kincannon is their leader. And they killed a cowboy from the Sleepy K. Trey. You know him? Young kid and—"

"I don't have time for such nonsense right now," Jenks said. "I may just have bitten off more than I can chew bringing her in here. I don't know for certain, but I suspect Pierre knows she is here."

"If he did, there'd be a mob outside demanding to string her up," Slocum said.

"They might be forming at the far end of town. Don't rightly know and don't care."

"Where are your deputies?"

Jenks snorted in disgust. "Yellow-bellies, the lot of them." He opened his desk drawer and showed three shiny badges. "They left, saying they didn't need to face down a lynch mob. By now they're probably in Coeur d'Alene."

"Why are you keeping her locked up? Have you charged her with anything?"

"Reckon I could say I think she's responsible for a couple murders."

"Look, Marshal. I got this from the pharmacist. He said Cora Kincannon has been giving it to Elspeth."

"What is it?" Jenks delicately dabbed his finger in the white powder inside the envelope Slocum shoved across the desk toward him.

"Laudanum powder. It's supposed to be mixed up in water and drunk. This is why Elspeth has been wandering aimlessly in a trance. Cora Kincannon has been giving it to her stepdaughter to give herself an alibi."

"You sayin' Cora went and killed Frank Kincannon?"

Slocum said nothing. That was exactly what he thought.

"Balderdash."

"She might not have done it herself, but you can bet that her loving brother-in-law did."

"Always was bad blood between Frank and Will," Jenks mused. Then he shook his head. "Don't make no never-mind. Not at the moment. Keeping *her* safe enough to stand trial is what bothers me most."

"If the mob finds out she's here, you won't hold them back with a single shotgun."

"Wouldn't be able to hold them back with a shotgun and three deputies," Jenks said. "But it's my job to try."

"The rustlers are killing men and blaming the wolves. I saw Trey die. At the railroad spur I told you about. They had another head of cattle to ship in freight cars. Trey said they carried the Rolling J brand."

"The colonel's been losing quite a few beeves," Jenks admitted. "But he's a former Army officer. He can take care of his own problems. I am only the town marshal, not the damned sheriff. Fact is, the cheapskates around here haven't ponied up money for a sheriff in well nigh two years.''

Slocum saw he wasn't getting anywhere. With all the proof in the world, he wouldn't budge Jenks. The marshal's stubborn insistence on dealing first with Elspeth spelled her death. If Pierre did not find out Elspeth was in the jail, Cora would. Or William. They had everything to lose with Elspeth alive, and everything to gain if she died.

''Keep her safe and sound,'' Slocum warned.

''Just don't go tellin' the world she's in there. You might tell Larry if you want.''

''Who?''

''The doctor,'' Jenks said tiredly. ''Miss Elspeth is looking peaked.''

''From all she's been through, she has a reason to,'' Slocum said. He wanted to look in on Elspeth again, to reassure her, but he didn't. The marshal's finger tapped restlessly on the double triggers that would send Slocum flying apart.

Slocum opened the door and looked up and down the street, to be sure no one was waiting to drygulch him.

''Slocum!'' called Jenks. ''For what it's worth, I believe you about Will Kincannon. Even about Cora. They're a real pair of stepped-on rattlers.''

''Thanks, Marshal,'' Slocum said, and then left. He had no intention of letting Elspeth stay in the jail. It would be a matter of time before someone spotted her and relayed the information to Pierre. The man had a hand in every rumor in Bannock.

Slocum headed for the general store. He had supplies to buy and plans to make for after sundown.

Waiting had been hard. Slocum had bided his time all day, wanting it to be dark so he could take Elspeth from the jail, and yet at the same time being thankful she was still safe. But now, even this small boon of fate came to an abrupt end.

He rocked forward in his chair and pushed his Stetson out of his eyes when he heard the mob tromping down the middle of the street. He glanced across at the jail. It seemed no different than it had a few seconds before— except it had gone from being a fortress of safety to a death trap for Elspeth Kincannon.

"The *loup-garou,* she is in the jail!" cried Pierre, leading the crowd. "She must die or more of our innocents will fall under her fangs!"

Slocum knew better than to try to argue or reason with the Cajun. The man had worked up the people of Bannock, and now either had to stay at their head or be trampled. It was as if Pierre had pushed a giant rock to the top of the mountain, and was now watching it tumble down the far side, turning from a single rock to an avalanche no one could stop.

Even with his shotgun, Jenks wasn't going to stop them. Slocum had to act on his own, even if it wasn't quite dark yet. He dashed around back of the general store, where two fresh horses waited. He rode one horse and led the other down the alley, then crossed and came up behind the jail. A single barred window showed Elspeth's cell. Grabbing two sticks of dynamite from the spare horse's saddlebags, Slocum went to the window and hissed to get Elspeth's attention.

"Who is it?" came her immediate reply. "I hear a crowd outside. Help me!"

"It's me, Slocum," he said. "Stand back from the window and shield yourself with the mattress. When the wall comes down, get out of there fast."

He worked feverishly to set the dynamite. Just dropping it would never blow the hole he wanted. He had to have the force of the blast go through the wall, shattering it. From the front of the jail he heard Pierre's stentorian demand for Elspeth to be turned out so she could be hung.

Slocum recoiled when a loud blast rocked him. Then he realized Marshal Jenks had fired both barrels of his shotgun to quiet the crowd. Slocum heard the lawman's voice as clearly as if he stood next to him in the alley.

"She's my prisoner! I don't let lynch mobs take anyone! Never have, never will!"

"Then it's your life, Marshal!" someone screamed.

"So be it!" Jenks said. Slocum pictured the man with his feet spread wide apart, two new shells in the shotgun, ready to cut down the first man stupid enough to enter the jail uninvited.

"She is the *loup-garou*, Marshal!" Pierre shouted. "All the while she is in your jail, there has been no more killing! She is free, men die with their throats ripped out! She is locked up, the killings they stop!"

This brought a loud cheer from the crowd. Slocum worked harder to dig down deep into the dirt so he could shove the twin sticks of dynamite against the jailhouse wall.

"John, hurry, hurry! They'll kill the marshal and be in here any second."

"Got it," Slocum said. "Stand clear." He had bought fast-burning black miner's fuse. One variety burned at a foot a minute. This burned at a foot every ten seconds. He cut a foot, shoved the blasting cap between the sticks, lit a lucifer, and applied it to the fuse.

"Here it comes!" he shouted, grabbing the horses' reins and jerking them away from the wall.

The explosion knocked him off his feet. Clinging desperately to the reins allowed him to regain his balance quickly. He spun and stared in disbelief at the wall. The explosion had cracked the wall, but hadn't blown it down.

On the far side of the jail, Pierre shouted for them to

rush past Jenks. The rumble of the shotgun told Slocum time was running out. He grabbed the lariat from his saddle and looped it around the iron bars in the window.

"John, please!" screamed Elspeth.

"Help it along," he told her. His horse snapped the rope taut and began pulling. The weakened wall finally gave and tumbled outward, Elspeth falling amid the chunks of concrete, stone, and clattering iron bars.

"Get up," Slocum ordered. "We've got a lot of riding to do—fast."

He reached down and grabbed her arm. Pulling hard, he hoisted her into the saddle. As he did so, he saw Pierre and four men from the lynch mob rounding the corner of the jail.

"There he is! He helps the *loup-garou* escape! Kill them both! Use the silver bullets!"

Slocum bent low and put his spurs to his horse's flanks. The animal rocketed from the alley as a hail of bullets tore past Slocum's head. He chanced a look to his right and saw Elspeth falling back, struggling to control her horse.

"Elspeth!" he shouted. Slocum jerked back on the reins, and his horse dug in its back hooves, sending up a curtain of choking dust. He wheeled about to see her fighting to get free of the horse.

Someone in the crowd had shot the horse. Whether it was only a lucky shot or superb marksmanship, Slocum neither knew nor cared. Pierre and his kill-crazy followers were narrowing the gap between them and Elspeth.

Slocum raced back down the alley, wheeled again in the tight space, and reached down for the woman.

"Get up behind me. It's our only chance!"

She started to protest. A shot from the crowd parted her hair, sending her staggering backward. Slocum edged his horse over, grabbed the woman's arm, and dragged her across his horse's rump.

"Here we go!" he cried. The horse took off, Elspeth fighting to stay in the uncomfortable position.

Slocum wished the escape could have gone better, but when he reached the end of the alley and saw only clear ground ahead, he knew they had made it.

But the question still burned in his mind now that he and Elspeth were safe. What was he supposed to do now?

17

"What do we do now, John?" Elspeth asked. She scooted around behind him, getting her seat. Her arms circled his waist as she clung tightly to him. For such a wispy-looking woman she had a lot of strength, Slocum thought.

"I don't know. We're running out of places to hide," he said. "About the only place we might go for help is Dr. Talbot."

"That'll be dangerous," Elspeth said. "The entire town is hunting for us."

Slocum didn't mince words. "They'd kill me and never notice, but it's *you* they want. Pierre's whipped them into a killing frenzy, and nothing will stop them until they've spilled enough blood—if there ever is enough blood for a lynch mob."

"John, what's going on? I can't understand any of it," she said. She started to cry, then caught herself and showed the steel center he had noticed in her so often.

"We need to get rid of your uncle and stepmother."

"I can't believe she's not my mother. Why didn't someone tell me? Why didn't Papa?"

"Every family can be ashamed of some relatives and

what they've done. This must be the Kincannon secret." Slocum shied away from mentioning what he'd read in the water-soaked family bible.

"There's no shame dying in childbirth," Elspeth said. "Do you think Cora hates me because I'm not her own flesh-and-blood daughter?"

"Frank Kincannon might have thought your mother's death was his fault," Slocum said. He wished he knew more about the events surrounding Elspeth's birth. Maybe Cora had been a midwife with an eye for a rich rancher, and had ingratiated herself by helping with the baby. This was something Slocum doubted they would ever learn.

Slocum doubled back on the trail, then found a rocky patch to trot his horse across. He did everything he could to throw off pursuit. Then he made his way back slowly toward Bannock, curving in a wide arc to avoid any direct pursuit. Dr. Talbot was the only chance he saw for getting away. The surgeon was cranky and profane, but had shown downright tenderness toward Elspeth. Slocum thought he would help them now that they needed it. An hour after breaking Elspeth out of the jail, Slocum rode slowly toward the doctor's office.

"I can't tell if Talbot's got somebody with him," Slocum said. "Take cover across the street. Look for another horse. We're not going to get far if we both weigh down one horse much longer." He patted his horse on the neck, and then waited to be sure Elspeth was obeying.

Bannock seemed deserted. He guessed those who'd remained after all that had happened were in a posse hunting Elspeth and him down. Slocum sidled up to Talbot's surgery and saw the office door standing ajar. He was glad he had been cautious. Someone was in the office with Talbot.

But Slocum didn't understand what was happening.

"You fool, you imbecile, you *tracked* me. You knew what would happen if you ever found me."

"Get back. I have this charm! It is blessed by the Virgin Mary!"

"Fake, just like your bullets."

A shot rang out, then another, and another. Slocum acted. He spun around, kicked the door open, and stood with his six-shooter leveled at the damnedest scene he had ever seen in his born days.

Dr. Talbot had pinned Pierre's shoulders to the floor with his knees. But the contemptuous ease the doctor showed toward the Cajun wasn't what started Slocum. It was the feral look on Talbot's face—and the blood dripping from his mouth. He had ripped out Pierre's throat with one savage jerk of his head.

"You . . ." Slocum was at a loss for words. He saw two bullet holes in the middle of Talbot's chest, gunpowder burns forming a star pattern around each hole showing how close Pierre had been to Talbot when he fired.

"I wish you hadn't seen this, Slocum. I liked you."

Slocum fired twice, each round slamming hard into Talbot's body. The impact knocked the doctor over his desk and sent him sprawling. But Slocum saw Talbot had not been killed. He struggled to get to his feet.

Slocum's mind raced. He reached to his shirt pocket, hating himself for being so superstitious. Taking the silver bullet Frank Kincannon had given him before the start of the wolf hunt, Slocum knocked open the six-gun and slid it into a chamber.

"I liked you, Slocum. I did. But you'd be a fool like Pierre. You'd follow me from one kill to the next." Talbot lurched forward. Slocum lifted the gun and fired.

The expression on Talbot's face ran from shock to horror, and then to a curious pleasure. "That's a damned real silver bullet. You *did* believe. I'll be damned." With that Talbot crashed forward, arms outstretched.

Slocum backed from the office, blinking at what he thought he saw.

"John, what's wrong?" Elspeth came running up.

"More trouble. Talbot won't be able to help us—or anyone, for all that." He tried to stop her but she pushed past him, then backed away fast.

"How awful. A wolf killed Pierre! But how did it get into Dr. Talbot's surgery?"

"Too many questions," he told her, grabbing her by the arm. "We have to bail ourselves out of a really tight place." Slocum saw Pierre's swayback horse, and grabbed its reins, handing them to Elspeth. She mounted as he fetched his own horse. They retraced the path they had taken into Bannock, angling back toward the Sleepy K when they were far enough away that they weren't likely to run up on a posse.

"Where are we going?" Elspeth asked after they had ridden for some time. Without realizing it, Slocum headed for the railroad spur on the San Martino spread. That was the only definite evidence he had of any wrongdoing by William Kincannon. A case might be lodged against him for buying up the land under suspicious circumstances, but Slocum knew the real crime came in how he had forced the owners to sell rather than actually purchasing the ranches.

"I'm not sure what I can do. Trey was gunned down here. There must be some evidence we can use against your uncle." Slocum morosely thought it might be best for them to keep riding and let Cora and William Kincannon have their ill-gotten gains.

Something inside refused to let go of the need to see the pair punished for all they'd done. And Slocum still couldn't make any sense out of the drama enacted in Dr. Talbot's office.

"John, there. Along the ridge. A rider. He's spotted us."

"Damn," Slocum said. They could retreat to the Sleepy K and try to make a stand there, or they could do the prudent thing and just leave Montana. He chose neither. He put his spurs to his horse and galloped forward, shouting like a scalded Apache.

Elspeth was hard put to keep up on her broken-down mount. That suited Slocum just fine. What he had to do required fancy gunslinging, and he wanted her out of the line of fire. He wasn't even sure he could accomplish anything, but he had to try.

A bullet tore past his ear, coming from his right. Ducking low, he rode hell-bent for leather into the stand of trees ahead. He hoped Elspeth had the good sense to stay where she was and not get involved. He whipped out his rifle and dropped to the ground. The shot needed to take out the sniper was easy for him.

He squeezed the trigger, the Winchester bucked, and the rustler fell to the ground like a bag of potatoes.

"There's one who knows the proper way to die," Slocum muttered. He didn't know what Talbot's incredible vitality meant, but there was no time to ponder it now. The gunfire had brought three more rustlers.

With them rode William Kincannon.

Slocum got off a shot at Kincannon, but missed. Worse than missing, he revealed his position to the rustlers. Kincannon bellowed orders, and the men with him fanned out, thinking to stop Slocum before he potshotted any more of their number.

Slocum ran as hard as he could, then cut back toward Kincannon. This let him do a flanking movement on one rustler. Slocum got off another shot at the mounted Kincannon. All he accomplished was forcing the man to the ground. Then he had his hands full with the man he had outmaneuvered coming up on him.

A heated exchange emptied Slocum's Winchester. He laid the hot-barreled rifle on the ground and slid his Colt from its holster. The man coming after him could play it cagey and wait for his friends to reinforce his attack, or he could play the hero, thinking Slocum was out of ammo.

He played the hero. Then he played the corpse. Slocum nailed him twice in the face with the Colt before hitting on an empty cylinder.

Slocum cursed his bad luck. He had forgotten to reload after the gunfight in Talbot's office. Crouching, he worked to get his Colt reloaded, then searched his pockets for ammo for the rifle. He had six rounds left for each.

"An even dozen. Got to make each shot count," he said, then took off toward the spot where Kincannon had gone to ground.

Slocum wasn't sure what happened next. He was alone in the woods—then he had two men firing at him. He spun about as one slug left a fiery trail across his upper arm. He almost dropped his rifle in pain, but held on grimly. He took two steps, then crashed forward onto his face.

"I got him. I shot the bastard!"

"Careful. He's as tricky as a Cheyenne brave," warned the other. "If we go together we can see if you really plugged him."

"He's dead. I never miss," boasted the first rustler. That was his last tall tale. Slocum shot him between the eyes, flopped over, and brought up his rifle. The slug from the Winchester missed the second, warier man, but Slocum didn't miss with his six-gun.

The rustler bent double, half turned, and flopped against a tree. Slocum checked both men. Dead.

That left his score to settle with William Kincannon for all he had done to his brother and his niece. Finding the rustler proved harder than Slocum had thought. Kincannon had let his men flush out Slocum, but where had *he* gone?

Slocum checked the siding, thinking there might have been a handcar or some other conveyance for Kincannon to escape on. Pressing his ear to the rails told him nothing moved along this stretch of track. Prowling back and forth, Slocum combed every inch of land. He found a corral filled with maybe thirty head of Rolling J cattle, newly stolen and not yet with new brands. How Kincannon had run the brands was apparent by the branding irons scattered around. The Rolling J ended up the Circle Cross. And Kincannon had even been running his own brother's brand. The Sleepy K turned into a Boxed Diamond with a little care and a lot of bad intent.

"You're not going anywhere, Slocum. You're going to drop your rifle and six-shooter first, then—"

Slocum dived forward, kicking hard to get under the bottom rail of the corral. The cattle complained at this intrusion, forcing Slocum to be more alert about being kicked or stepped on than shot by William Kincannon.

When he had enough beef between him and the outlaw, Slocum peered over the back of one agitated cow.

"Doesn't much matter what you do, Slocum. Elspeth's going to end up with a bullet in her head." Kincannon stood with his six-shooter pressed against Elspeth's temple. "Then I'm gonna kill you for messing up the sweetest deal I ever saw."

"You bought up the land after scaring off the owners?"

"You know I did."

"You killed all those people?"

"Some, not all. The wolves gave me the idea after they killed a gent riding into town a few months ago. Use the timber wolves to chase off people, buy their spreads for next to nothing."

"You'd been rustling before that, hadn't you?"

"Of course, but I wasn't greedy. A few here and there gave me pocket money. Money Frank would never give me, his own brother!"

"So Cora told you the time was right for killing Frank and framing Elspeth?"

"Cora doesn't tell me anything. I tell *her*!"

Slocum doubted that. He had seen the two of them together enough to know Will Kincannon talked a big game but Cora had the brains. Kincannon would have been content to rustle a few cows now and then for poker money. Cora was far more ambitious—and greedy.

"Enough of this, Slocum," shouted Kincannon. "Get your ass out here right now. I want to see both your guns come out first."

"John, he'll kill you too!"

Kincannon laughed as he cocked the six-shooter he held at Elspeth's head. Slocum gauged a dozen factors at the same time. Windage, range, elevation, reaction time. He brought up his rifle and fired.

The picture burned itself into Slocum's brain. Kincannon's eyes went wide in surprise. He started to speak and couldn't. He tried to pull the trigger on his six-gun and end Elspeth's life.

All he succeeded in doing was to die.

"John," cried Elspeth, falling to her knees. "You shot him in the face! He's dead!"

"You would have been dead if I hadn't," Slocum said as he came up to her. "Me too. He wanted us both dead. Worked out in our favor this way." He nudged the body with the toe of his boot. "With all the evidence of rustling around here, the marshal's bound to come to the right conclusion."

"But he'll know Uncle Will didn't kill himself!"

"There are three dead rustlers back there. Marshal

Jenks can conjure up some wild story about how the gang had a falling out and shot each other. Maybe a rustler or two got away scot-free. That's for him to say.''

''It's all over then,'' Elspeth said in a monotone voice as if she couldn't believe it.

''Not yet,'' Slocum said grimly. ''There's still your stepmother to deal with. And I know just the way to get even.''

18

"Ready?" Slocum asked Elspeth. She nodded, her hair midnight black against her pale face. She seemed to have shrunk in on herself after her uncle had died at Slocum's hand.

"There's no other way to do this?" the woman finally asked. "This seems so . . . so awful."

Slocum remembered the details in the Kincannon family bible, and knew Cora Kincannon had used that history for her own ends. She would have let the girl she had raised from infancy die at the hands of a lynch mob—and all for nothing more than greed.

"There's no evidence against her," Slocum said. "With your uncle dead, she can claim it was all his doing. This might not be the only way, but it's the only way I can think of."

"Let's do it, then," Elspeth said in a small voice.

Slocum left her in shadows just beyond the ranch house. He dismounted and clomped up the front steps, then rapped loudly. He heard Cora Kincannon inside, rushing to see who was at the door.

"Oh, it's you," she said in a nasty voice. "What do you want?"

"Bad news, ma'am," Slocum said. "Elspeth's got away from jail. The marshal's hunting for her, but so far he's not had any luck."

"I know she's gone," Cora snapped. "I'm not a complete dolt."

"Uh," Slocum said, turning, then stopping as if hesitant to broach a delicate subject. "Marshal Jenks has an eyewitness who claims Elspeth really *is* a *loup-garou*. She ripped the throat out of Pierre, the Cajun fella, and then ran off. Don't put much credence to this, but Elspeth's supposed to have run off on all fours, like an animal."

"Like a wolf," Cora said in a choked voice. She stared at the bible, then jerked her attention back to Slocum.

"I reckon if any part of that's true, it might be she's snapped under the strain of losing her pa and all. She couldn't possibly be a werewolf. You'd've known it long ago."

"What do you mean snapped? You think she's become a lunatic?"

"Doc Talbot considered it a possibility. Said sometimes a woman's mind can change to accept real peculiar things, when she's distressed or taking odd drugs or even when she—"

"Taking drugs can do this?" Cora looked horrified.

"Surely can, ma'am. The doctor mentioned something about opium making people see things that aren't there, causing them to believe odd stories."

"Stories like that of the *loup-garou*?"

"But probably not in *her* case, ma'am. It would take years of hearing about being a *loup-garou* before anything like that could happen, and Miss Elspeth never even heard of a werewolf before that dead Cajun fella came to town."

"Pierre's dead?"

"That's what I heard. Night, ma'am," Slocum said, heading for the bunkhouse. He waited until Cora closed the door before signaling Elspeth. The woman drifted through the night like a ghost. Her feet made no sound as she crossed the yard and went up the steps. She opened the door and went in. As Slocum had instructed her, she left the door ajar so he could watch. He wasn't going to lose Elspeth because Cora panicked and ventilated her with a gun lying around the house.

"Mother," Elspeth said in a ghostly voice. "I have come for you. I have found my true nature." She walked to the bible and flipped it open. "I am not the first Kincannon to be a *loup-garou.*"

"No, dear, wait. It's not like you think." Cora backed up, hand at her throat as if this would protect her against a werewolf. "The drugs I gave you did this. Laudanum in your water. I gave it to you so your uncle and I could . . . so we could make you think you were a *loup-garou.* You're not. You're perfectly normal."

"Why would you ever want to put on such a charade, Mother? No, I *am* a creature of the night. I find the thought of tearing out your throat so tasty. Blood excites me."

"Elspeth!" Cora Kincannon cried. "Listen! *We* killed some of the men. We used things we hid out in the toolshed. There's no such thing as a *loup-garou.* Your father was foolish to believe there was. He was such a fool."

"And you will be my foolish dinner," Elspeth said, moving around the chair in an attempt to corner her stepmother.

"No!" Cora screamed, and dodged past Elspeth, running to the door. She collided with Slocum just outside. "Save me! She's crazy! She's trying to kill me! She thinks she really is a werewolf!".

"You mean she really *did* kill Barnsley and her pa?"

Slocum recoiled in mock horror, turned, and started to run.

"Wait, save me! Help me against her, Slocum! I'll make you part owner of the Sleepy K! Will and I have plenty to go around!"

"Nothing I want to get tangled in. Maybe the marshal can help," Slocum said, vanishing behind a woodpile. He ducked down and circled, coming back to the end of the porch. Elspeth walked slowly from the house, then snarled exactly like a wolf. If Slocum hadn't known it was the woman, he would have gone for his gun to bag another hide.

"Noooo!" Cora shrieked, and jumped on Pierre's swayback horse. She got the old horse moving by furiously kicking him with her heels. Cora Kincannon headed for town.

"You think she will find Marshal Jenks?" Elspeth asked Slocum.

"She will. I suspect he and the posse aren't too far down the road."

"I'd feel sorry for her if she hadn't killed all those people," Elspeth said. "Still, killing's not so bad if you do it to survive."

"What's that?" Slocum's eyes narrowed as he stared at the woman.

"We kill cattle for food, don't we? You killed all those wolves. It was all a matter of survival for us." Elspeth went back into the house, humming a jaunty tune. Slocum followed, not sure what to say.

"This is the proof, isn't it?" Elspeth said, leafing through the Bible. "So many of my ancestors were also *loup-garou.*"

"You'd better hide. I hear horses," Slocum said uneasily. "That's got to be the marshal and his posse. They're still hungry to string you up without a trial."

"Thank you for all you've done for me, John." She

bent and kissed him, then gave his cheek a quick lick. Laughing, Elspeth dashed off just as the marshal, Cora Kincannon, and a half-dozen men came into the house.

"Slocum, figured you'd be here. Don't know why," Jenks said sourly.

"Evening, Marshal. Mrs. Kincannon." Slocum tipped his hat to her, as if this was the first he had seen of her. Jenks noted it, but Cora didn't.

"I didn't mean to turn her into a werewolf," Cora prattled. "Will and I killed two of the cowboys. We used poles with wolf feet on them to stand back and put paw prints into the ground. And Will took a bear trap and glued wolf teeth to it. Knock a man unconscious, spring the trap on his throat, then pull. It looks like a wolf bite that way." Cora was babbling, her fear coloring her words. "You *are* going to protect me from her."

"Elspeth?"

"She's a real *loup-garou*. She is a wolf and kills men."

"You confessed to a passel of murders, Mrs. Kincannon. Who's Elspeth supposed to have killed?"

"I gave her laudanum to fog her mind. Will thought it would be easy to blame the murders on her. With her out of the way, he would inherit the Sleepy K and we'd get married and we'd be rich."

"Mrs. Kincannon, who are you saying you killed?"

"Deputy Hines. Will killed him and put his vest in Elspeth's room. I don't know what the bitch did with it. Hid it somewhere. And all the others. All of them. We killed them."

"You're confessing to all this in front of me, the posse, and God?" Jenks asked, stunned.

"Save me from her! She'll kill me like she did Barnsley!"

"So you think your daughter killed your foreman?" asked the marshal.

"She's my stepdaughter. I'd never spawn a creature like her! Save me, Marshal. You have to!" Froth flecked Cora Kincannon's mouth. It took two strong men from the posse to subdue her as she fought.

"Never seen the like," Jenks said. "What she and Will did went beyond greed. Imagine killing your own husband and trying to pin it on your daughter."

"Stepdaughter," Slocum said. "I reckon you might find papers in Seth Fenstermacher's office that will shed some light on all that. Just supposing, Marshal, just supposing." Slocum stared down the marshal.

"Marshal, lookee here at what we found. Right where Miz Kincannon said they were too." One of the men from the posse held up two five-foot poles with wolf paws tied to the ends. And another tried to open a bear trap outfitted with a wolf jaw and teeth.

"So danged powerful I can't even open it, Marshal. Imagine this contraption snappin' shut on your neck." The man held up the bloody murder device in awe.

"Does all this clear Miss Elspeth?" Slocum asked. "You heard her stepmother say she was drugging her, just as I told you. Ask the pharmacist. And Will Kincannon was buying up land and rustling cattle."

"If I go out to this railroad spur, you figure I'd find evidence of rustling and that Will's responsible for it all?"

"Could be," Slocum said.

"Get her back to town, man. Slocum here's gonna show us where the rustlers shipped their cattle on the Northern Pacific."

Slocum patted his shirt pocket. He carried a wad of greenbacks big enough to bankroll a good stud farm over in Oregon. He had always liked the spotted Appaloosas. The money Elspeth had given him would go a long way toward a decent herd.

Even as he traced the outline of the money, he remembered the silver bullet he had carried there so long—the silver bullet that had taken Dr. Talbot's life after ordinary lead ones wouldn't. Slocum wondered why Frank Kincannon had had such a bullet, unless he'd thought he might have to use it.

Had Cora so twitched his mind so that he'd believed his own daughter capable of being a *loup-garou*? Slocum would never know, not with the Kincannon brothers dead and Cora gibbering in a jail cell. It hadn't taken much for the judge to declare her crazy as a bedbug.

"She'll be well taken care of, John. I'll see to that," Elspeth said. He jerked around. "Cora," the woman said softly. "You were thinking about her. I bear her no real ill will."

"That's mighty forgiving of you. I don't think I could forgive like that, but then I'm not much for church-going."

"Neither am I," Elspeth said. She took Slocum's arm and walked with him to the edge of the woods near the ranch house. "So much has happened on the Sleepy K. I won't be sorry to leave it."

"You heading back East to live with your cousins?" he asked.

"Where did you get that notion?"

"Heard Marshal Jenks mention it," Slocum said.

"I don't belong back East. I love Montana. It is so open and so free. I can do what I want. I can be free here. No, the money from the Sleepy K—and the other ranches, since Uncle Will bought them legitimately—will give me a nice nest egg."

They walked in silence for a few more minutes. The sun began settling down over the horizon, lighting the twilight with brilliant streaks of orange and yellow intermingled with snow-white clouds. He understood how hard it would be to leave this part of the country for St.

Louis or any of the crowded cities of the East.

"I belong here, just as you do, John."

"I can leave in the morning," he said.

"No, that's not a good idea, John. The times together were special. Let's keep them as memories. You ought to ride on out now. While you can."

"While I can?"

"Oh, you might invent reasons to stay," she said in a husky voice.

"That's not what you meant. I can hear it in your words."

"Let's just say that I was outraged when I found Quint was fetching the laudanum for Cora."

Slocum took a deep breath, considered kissing her good-bye, then decided against it. He left without another word. As he mounted, Slocum heard the shrill mocking call of a wolf from the woods where he and Elspeth had just been.

He knew then why Frank Kincannon had fashioned the silver bullet. Slocum put his spurs to his horse's flanks and trotted off in the opposite direction. With luck he could be halfway to Coeur d'Alene before the horse tired too much to continue.